*Some walks seem to take* about the destination. *Every time my friends and I, as teens,* had walked to Comiskey Park it seemed an eternity. *My walk to the big scary house this night, however, seemed as though I had been shot from a cannon. It was just as well — there was a chilly, stinky wind blowing off the river and I only wore my suit jacket and hat for protection.*

*Once at the door, I could hear a radio playing. I swallowed my spit and knocked as if I belonged there.*

*The little door within the door opened and a beady pair of eyes looked at me suspiciously. "What do you want?" asked the voice that belonged to the eyes.*

*"I've got your comic books," I heard myself saying. I had not planned to say it — it just came out of my mouth.*

*"Comic books?" asked the voice.*

*"Sure. One load of 'Archie,' and a whole box full of 'Casper the Friendly Ghost.'"*

*"Casper?"*

*"The friendliest ghost you know. Come on, I got a ton of deliveries to finish tonight. You want 'em or not?"*

*"Let me see those things." And the door flew open.*

*I didn't wait for any further comic book chit chat. I yanked the guy out by the arms and landed an uppercut right on the tip of his chin — the sweet spot. He went down like cooked noodles.*

To Karan M.—

# THE HONDURAN OPAL

### BY

### Bill Telfer

MUCH LOVE

~ Bill T.

# A CANARYVILLE MYSTERY
(CBM-1)

First Canaryville Books edition January, 2020

Published by
Canaryville Books
P.O. Box 386
Elwood, IL 60421

Cover painting by Brenda Alexsandra
brendaalexa11@gmail.com

Back cover photo of author by Nikki Shell

Special thanks
Nichól Brinkman
https://www.instagram.com/pink_cheeks_studios/

*This book is a work of fiction.  Names, characters, places, and incidents either are the products of the author's imagination or are used fictitiously, and any resemblance to actual events or persons, living or dead, is entirely coincidental.*

ISBN 978-1-79486-353-8

The name "Canaryville Books" and the Canaryville logo are trademarks of Taillefer Arts.

Printed in the United States of America

*For Marge*

# Chapter One

Why I was experiencing this flashback from my life – right at this particular moment – is difficult to say. I have my theories. But lying there on my back, covered in sweat, I was being revisited by one of the worst memories of my life. It was of the one and only defeat I'd suffered in the ring. And it was from a knockout punch – the only one I'd ever received. I was flat on my back and waking up right around the time the ref was saying "six" or "seven." I wanted to get up, to get on my feet and end the count. But my muscles wouldn't obey the commands from my brain.

There was the ref swinging his arm as he counted. And there was Orangutan, bouncing up and down in a neutral corner behind the ref and looking as pleased as could be. And there I was: dazed, squirming, and grunting – and going nowhere.

This had been a rematch. A friendly one, or so I was naïve enough to think. I'd first officially gotten into the ring with Orangutan Gibbon, that red-headed beast, several months before. We'd been pals, workout buddies up at Cully's Gym. But at the conclusion of our first real Heavyweight match, I'd broken his nose – had given him a profile like Barrymore's.  So when he'd asked for a rematch in the spirit of friendly competition, I didn't see how I could refuse him.

Since I'd started boxing back in high school, I'd built a reputation:  no one could lay a glove on me, usually.  But the night of the rematch, Orangutan had done his homework.  He let me bob and weave just out of his reach for three rounds, giving me false confidence.  Then at the top of the fourth round, he came out of his corner with a different look in his eye.  That left of his seemed to come out of nowhere.  And all of a sudden I was flat on my back.

Old Orangutan and I stayed friendly after that but, sad to say, we were no longer pals.

That experience matured me as a fighter, and no one ever knocked me out again the rest of my time in the ring.  But the memory of that one knockout remained as one of my very worst memories.

So, as I was saying, that's the image that was now in my mind.  I felt exactly as if Orangutan had just clobbered me again.  Only I wasn't in the ring.  I was in a bed.  And there was no ref, no Orangutan, no screaming crowd.

I was next to a female.

And she was running her bright red fingernail slowly up my chest, on its way to my chin.

I glanced over at Maeve Hoolihan. The sun through the open bedroom window gave her naked hips a shiny, sweaty sheen. We were both naked now. It was amazing how quickly that could happen. The only remaining evidence that either of us had ever owned clothing were the underpants looped around Maeve's left ankle. She had a cigarette going between her lips – the bright red lipstick (which almost perfectly matched her fingernail polish) smeared here and there.

When that fingernail reached my chin she attempted to tickle me under it, but the nail only scraped at my neck. It didn't hurt exactly, so I just clammed up about it. But I didn't pretend to laugh, either.

We lay like this, in post-coital reverie for a few minutes. Then Maeve dragged deeply on her cigarette, removed it with the hand that had been trying to tickle, blew a stream of smoke in the direction of the ceiling light, and spoke.

"You're so funny." Then she giggled that insipid way she had, like a funhouse clown, when she was trying to force a light mood. I usually think I'm a million laughs, but I didn't see what was so funny now, and I wondered what exactly she was giggling about. Before I could ask, however, she added, "I'll bet you're hungry, I know I'm starved."

I was about to agree that I was indeed famished, when there was the slam of a car door.

"Oh Christ – it's Pete!"

We sprang off the bed, terrified alley cats with a slavering bulldog bearing down.

I never shy from a fight; anyone who knows me will tell you that. Pete was nearly ten years older than me, but he was nearly a foot taller and almost twice as wide. I've fought bigger men, but you add to his size his inevitable reaction to finding someone tupping his wife – well, that was a recipe for violence I was not in a mood to sample. (And I'd seen him angrily crush beer bottles in those big mitts of his.)

"Oh, God! Oh, God!" Maeve whispered hoarsely, the cigarette dangling wildly from her lower lip, as she scuttled about scooping up loose clothing items. "He was on his way to South Bend, I swear, Bobber!"

"Don't say my name!" I whispered back, just as hoarsely. "We don't need him hearing you say my name!"

I scooped up my own clothing, brogans included, and tumbled out the window into the freshly budding cotoneasters. All scraped up from the little bastard branches, I lay very still for a couple minutes. The window faced the small backyard and alley beyond, so I wasn't in imminent danger of someone spotting a naked man lying in the Hoolihan's bushes. I heard Maeve go into the bathroom and shut the door. I heard Pete announce his presence and heard Maeve reply, all cool as Sonja Henie shaking hands with Hitler. Soon she came out of the bathroom, and their conversation began, muffled in the kitchen. From his tone, it did not appear that Pete was wise to any shenanigans.

I did not wait around straining to hear his reason for not being in South Bend like he was supposed to be. Struggling into my clothing in record time, I awkwardly emerged from the bushes – hoping I had not been observed by anyone – and headed down the alley for home.

Home was only a few houses down and across that alley, on the same block.

I still called that house my home, anyway. I had grown up there. But, increasingly, it didn't feel much like home anymore. It was Ma's house, and it happened to be where I was currently sleeping since returning from the war. And the arrangement had become more and more intolerable.

The house itself was a modest one-and-a-half-story bungalow, purchased by my parents when I was still a kid. It sat smack dab in the middle of a south Chicago Irish neighborhood called Canaryville. Growing up, my friends and I sometimes wondered about that name. No adult ever bothered to explain it to us. We sure as hell never saw any damned canaries. Just a bunch of Micks with the occasional Croat or Serb thrown in, just for fun.

We were often treated to horrific odors from a rendering plant a mile or so from us. But because the reek was so ever present, we were all used to it. Most days.

Pa had worked in a nearby steel mill, managed to get promoted to foreman over the years, and retired – just in time to get a fat pension and to die of a heart attack less than a year later. I had just finished high school at the time of his death. Ma now lived (and had been able to live for years) off that godsend of a pension, and it gave her the freedom to get into, and make plenty of, trouble. Following Pa's death, The Depression had been busy ruining plenty of folk all around us. And while we did not remain completely unscathed, that pension (and its bank which somehow stayed solvent) really saved our asses.

The little bungalow currently needed a fresh coat of paint. And some plumbing work. And a thousand other things that houses need. And these were things I had been happy to do in Pa's absence. And as my boxing career began to flourish in my late teens and throughout my twenties, I always found time to put in the storm windows or re-grout the bathroom tile, etcetera.

But then that damn war broke out. And it wrecked everything. Well, it wrecked my boxing career, that's for sure.

Nobody had wanted to go to war. Then Pearl Harbor got bombed. Then everybody wanted to go to war. I know it wasn't really that simple, but it sure seemed so at the time. At home I was becoming a Prince of the Boxing Ring, winning card after card (at six foot two, I vacillated between two hundred five and two hundred fourteen pounds – always a Heavyweight), collecting some healthy purses, and climbing the ladder slowly so that some national title fights seemed in my future. So as I listened, at the age of twenty-nine, to the war news from Europe, I worried about my career and what being forced to join the service by conscription or enlistment (through social pressure) might do to it. But after Pearl Harbor? I held out not even a couple months and enlisted for a three year hitch. I had war fever. We all did.

So when I got out, at age thirty-three, the Chicago Boxing Commission gave me some cock and bull story about how I was now an "old man" where boxing was concerned. I never got the straight dope – all I knew was they refused to renew my license. I was now a has-been.

So now it was the following spring and I was zeroing in on my thirty-fourth birthday. I had no job. I was fucking our neighbor's wife (the better part of a decade my senior). And my ma's house needed painting.

Entering through the rear gate which opened onto the alley, I walked up the flagstone walk which bisected our backyard. Ma had been doing the wash (it must have been Monday) and the wet, white sheets flapped in the May sunshine, tickling my arm as I neared the house.

Hoping Ma was in the basement I planned to avoid the outside cellar door, quietly sneak up to my tiny dormered bedroom built under the sloping roof of the second floor, and dig some change out of my mason jar. I would then make my way, on foot, down the street to Tim's Tap. There I would listen to the Sox game on Tim's radio with whomever else was hiding out that fine day, and make it back home long after Pete Hoolihan was really on the road to South Bend. That was the plan.

But Ma was waiting for me in the kitchen.

I stopped dead in my tracks when I saw her. There's no doubt that I had the guiltiest of guilty looks on my kisser.

"Oh, sure, and it's himself," said Henrietta Maxwell (nee Henrietta Hart). "Out for a stroll this fine day, are ya? A real Nature Boy, wearin' twigs in his hair." Mortified, I felt for and pulled out part of the cotoneaster bush from behind my ear. I awkwardly dropped the offending twig into the kitchen garbage.

At four feet eleven, Ma was the most terrifying woman in America. Her once jet black hair had now mostly gone to gray, streaked occasionally with black. But her blue eyes were still clear and sparkled like diamonds, and they didn't miss much.

"I was just down at Jobie's, Ma," I lied. "He's going to order that paint for us. He can get it for us for a fraction of what they want at the hardware store. As soon as it arrives, I'll get out the ladder and – "

"Oh Kee-rist," said Ma. "Stow that shite of yours, willya? I want to talk to you. And this ain't about painting the Goddamned house. Sit down there!"

"Can I pour myself a glass of milk first?"

"No. I said sit."

I sat. Without a glass of milk.

"I am thirty-three years old, you know."

"I know how Goddamned old you are, Roderick." I became known as "Bobber" after I started boxing (and I showed a talent for "bobbing and weaving" and footwork), and now everyone called me "Bobber." Except Ma. She absolutely hated my nickname and refused to acknowledge it.

"Roderick," she said, sitting down in the chair opposite me at the kitchen table, "there's an issue I want to address." This was killing me. I had never had such a taste for a glass of milk. If I'd been at Tim's right then, I'd have passed on a beer and asked them to hook me up with the moo juice.

I sighed deeply. "If it's not about painting the house, then what, Ma? I always chip in plenty for our expenses – do you want more, is that it?" I knew in my gut that wasn't it.

Ma folded her hands together on the tabletop and mustered her patience. No small task for her. I could tell she really wanted what she was about to say to be taken seriously.

"Okay, I know yer an adult, Roderick. Technically. I know also that you've served yer country in two theaters o' war." She pronounced "Theaters" as "tee-uh-ters" with her brogue. And it was true. After VE Day, my division was sent across the Atlantic on a troop transport and we all thought we were going home. But in the middle of the night, we went through the Panama Canal and found ourselves stationed in the Philippines – where we remained for the rest of the war! "And, Lord knows, I died a towzen detts every second you were away." She crossed herself, paused, then continued. "But. But there's been talk. Mabel told me."

I breathed slowly, trying to contain my own patience. "For the love of Christ, Ma. What's Mabel been sayin' now?"

Rather than answer me directly, she said, "Is there something goin' on between you and Maeve Hoolihan, Roderick? Like for instance, where were you comin' from just now? Because you sure as hell weren't comin' from the direction of Jobie's. You were comin' from the direction of the Hoolihan's. I saw yer walkin' down the alley – through the window."

My face reddened. I could feel the back of my ears getting hot. I stared down at the tabletop utterly ashamed. After stammering a bit, I said. "Honestly, Ma, it's really nothin'."

"Nothin'?" she asked. I hadn't seen her this angry in a long time, and that's saying a lot. "So, if Pete Hoolihan shows up at our front door with a shotgun, or maybe a gang of his plumbin' buddies with lead pipes, is that what I'm supposed to say? 'Aw, Pete, Roderick says it was nothin'.'"

I couldn't take it anymore. I stood up. I didn't get angry back, I wouldn't dare. But I did plan to make my escape.

"I can't listen to this, Ma. There's nothing going on between me and Maeve. She just likes to talk. She wants to hear my war stories. Okay? I'm gonna go listen to the Sox play down at Tim's."

I made a move toward the stairs that led up to my dormer. But Henrietta wasn't done with me.

"Roderick," she said. "Let's not even pretend I believe ya even a little. The whole neighborhood knows what that woman is about. I should go over there and put me boot up her hoo-ha. But I won't. Yer right. Yer a grown man. But you have ta figure some things out. Like where yer gonna live, what yer gonna do. 'Cause I'm tellin' ya, boyo, you ain't gonna be carryin' on like this under my roof. I love ya. But I'm startin' ta feel ashamed of ya. I didn't raise a layabout, but that's what that war did to ya. Well – undo it or leave."

And without waiting for my reaction, she slammed out the backdoor to attend to the wash.

Petulantly, I poured myself a glass of milk and took it upstairs. I sat at the foot of my bed and made the springs squeak, sipping at the milk. It was cold but tasted slightly sour. I drank it anyway.

Over in the corner of this tiny room, on the far side of my bed, was the punching bag Pa had attached to the low ceiling so many years ago. I must have been about seven, no more than eight.

The bag made its appearance in my life this way: I had been walking home from school when I came upon a fight. Two of the Croation kids had my friend Casey on the ground and were pounding the shit out of him. The usual crowd of screaming kids had gathered. The Croation boys were a year older than Casey and me, but I was already fairly big, and I flew into them with a rage I'd never felt before, fists windmilling wildly. I don't remember who I hit or where. But the older boys ran off quickly and I helped Casey to his feet.

Not long after that, Ma got an angry phone call from Mrs. Arambasich accusing me of bloodying the lip of her poor little Dale (the lousy snitch).

After she hung up, Ma let me tell my side of the story. And, to her credit, she believed me. But I had to explain the whole thing again to Pa when he got home. He too listened and believed. But he also said he didn't want those Arambasich kids and their buddies to gang up on me one day. He told me to never walk home by myself if I could help it. And the next day he began teaching me to fight – the right way, but dirty tricks, too, should I need them. He also installed that punching bag.

So I looked at the bag now as it hung there forlornly. I could see a tiny spider had attached a web from the bag to the ceiling. The bag had not seen any action in years. Certainly not since I had gotten home from the army.

And as peeved as I was at Ma right now, she was right of course. I'd let Maeve corner me down at the park a few weeks back. In retrospect, she probably had been stalking me like I was a damned quail. There had been an invitation to tell her "all about the war." But I knew why she was really inviting me over. I also knew that Pete had always been a good friend of our family's. When I was in the service, he came over and fixed Ma's shower for free. And that was only one of his many kindnesses since Pa's death. Did I think at all of him when I accepted that invitation? Well, I can't say his face didn't flash through my brain, but not for very long. I hadn't gotten laid very much since I'd gotten back and here was an easy opportunity with an attractive married acquaintance who made no bones about her sexual appetite. The consensus was that Pete, while he may have suspected at times, knew very little of Maeve's dalliances. And what he didn't know wouldn't hurt him, I told myself. So if other guys I knew had taken advantage of her invitations, why shouldn't I?

Before the war, I couldn't imagine myself being so numb and jaded. But now I was clearly letting myself wander into Who Gives a Fuck Land. It wasn't a good feeling. Yet even with this realization, I knew that, given the opportunity, I would probably fuck Maeve again. That wasn't a good feeling either.

I finished the slightly sour milk and dug out a handful of change, enough for a few beers, and got ready to head down to Tim's

I heard the sound of conversation out in the backyard. Ma was talking to someone. The hairs on the back of my neck did a little rumba at the thought that it might be Pete. But, no, it was a male and female and they sounded nothing like the Hoolihans. I wasn't sure who these people were. The backdoor opened and Ma was saying, "Come in, folks, come in." Then her voice got louder as she yelled up the stairway, "Roderick! Come down! We got company!"

I poured my handful of change into my pants pocket and galloped down the steps, two at a time, my manner since childhood.

Ma had brought the guests into the living room. It was Mr. and Mrs. O'Kief from two blocks down. They were old church friends of my parents. I'd gone to grade school over at St. Michael's with their oldest daughter Bridget. Unlike Ma and Pa, who only had me (I was enough), the O'Kiefs had a ton of kids. I think Ma had babysat for all of 'em.

"Hello, folks," I said as I entered the room. But I cut my greeting short. I could tell by their ashen expressions that something was very wrong.

"Let's all sit down," said Ma. The O'Kiefs took our gray davenport and Ma sat on the piano bench, but faced into the room not towards the piano. I waited for everyone else, then I perched on the edge of my ass on Pa's old easy chair so I wouldn't sink into it.

"Would you folks like a cool drink? Donal, Kathy? I just made some lemonade."

"Oh, no, Henrietta, thank you," said Mrs. O'Kief, with a dismissive gesture. A strand of her graying hair fell across her brow, and she brushed it back absently. "We just want to say what we've got to say and move on."

Ma looked at me. She and I were a family unit in this setting, a united front, our conversation of before forgotten for the moment. "The O'Kiefs are in some distress, Roderick. Go ahead, folks, finish what you started to tell me outside."

"It's our Erin, Bobber," said Donal O'Kief, his face a mask of anxiety. "You remember Erin, right?"

"Sure," I said apprehensively. Erin was one of their younger children; when I'd been in eighth grade (St. Michael's had all eight grades in one building) she'd only been in first. A cuter kid you'd never want to see – red hair in pigtails and freckles, she was the darling of the neighborhood. I hadn't seen much of her in years, though, and had no idea what she'd been up to. I was positive I was not going to like what Mr. O'Kief was going to say next.

"Well, she's missing." He said it like the bad news it was. He just wanted to get it over with. Mrs. O'Kief covered her eyes in her hands and sobbed quietly.

"Oh, no," I said stupidly, unable to think of anything else. "How… when did you realize this?"

"We've been unable to reach her for a couple of weeks now. You knew she moved downtown?"

"No, I didn't know that."

"Right after the New Year," Mrs. O'Kief sniffed behind her fingers. "She got a job."

"Job," Mr. O'Kief grunted bitterly. "She had a job at that dress shop. Perfectly good job."

In defense of her daughter, Mrs. O'Kief said in a tremble, "Oh, Donal, the girl was twenty-seven. She just wanted to move out on her own, get a better job. Anyone wants that now."

"She should have married Pip when she had the chance," Mr. O'Kief muttered bitterly. I didn't know who this Pip was, but I could tell from Mrs. O'Kief's glare at her husband that she didn't think much of Pip.

"So, she's missing and you can't reach her," I said, trying to help these poor folks along. Bickering over missed opportunities to marry jerks was not going to help them. "Where was she staying? Where was she working? What does her new boss say about all this?"

"Hah," Mr. O'Kief grumbled, looking at a spot on our living room carpet I had made with grape juice at the age of twelve. He, of course, knew nothing of this spot's origin, but it helped him focus himself through the ordeal.

"We don't know any of that," said Mrs. O'Kief, dabbing at her cheeks with an ossified tissue she'd been clutching. "She wouldn't tell us. She did not leave on good terms with us. It was horrible."

"We just want to go door to door in the neighborhood," said Mr. O'Kief, still staring at the stain, "to see if anyone – anyone – has any idea where she went."

"What do you mean, you can't reach her," Ma broke in, "if she didn't tell ya where she was going?"

"We have one phone number," said Mrs. O'Kief. "Erin gave it to her sister Peggy. It was supposed to be the number of this fella she was seeing in the city. Peg wasn't supposed to give it to us, but when Erin stopped calling Peggy on the phone, Peg got scared and gave it to us. But no one ever answers."

"What was this guy's name?" I asked.

"Peggy says it was Vaughn Picout," said Mr. O'Kief, shaking his fist suddenly. "Let me tell ya, Bobber, that Vaughn Picout better hope I never get my hands on him – " he broke off.

A faint echo of a memory told me I had heard that name somewhere a long time ago, but it could have been one of those false memories. I kept this to myself for the moment. Now did not seem like a good time to be spouting off with hazy memories that might not even be real.

Before they left, they told us a little more. They had sent Erin's older brother Colin into the city to contact the police. But the cops had sent Colin stomping angrily back home, saying if an adult woman didn't want to see her family that was no indication that there'd been any foul play. I'd been drinking with that hothead Colin O'Kief on many occasions, and I was certain he had only aggravated the cops from the moment he'd stepped into the precinct station.

"How did Colin know which precinct to visit?" I asked.

Mrs. O'Kief blinked as if the question were irrelevant, then said, "Oh, well, Peggy knew the area where Erin was supposed to be working. The north Loop someplace."

"Well, that's something," I said.

We assured the O'Kiefs that we hadn't heard a thing about Erin, but we'd be sure to pass along to them any information that did come our way.

They thanked us and moved on with their sad sweep of the neighborhood.

"Those poor bastards," said Ma after they'd left.

"Poor Erin," I said. "I hope they find her. Hey, what was with that Pip she was going with? What was he like?"

"A bloody numbskull," said Ma. "Some dumb bunny she took up with. I tink he sold chalk."

"Chalk?" I asked. But Ma was done with the conversation and headed back out to deal with the wash.

I wended my way over to Tim's.

The walk to the tavern was bright and sunny enough. But somehow the sunshine made me crabby this day. Opening the screen door of Tim's, however, being enveloped by its darkness and boozy cigarette aromas, made me feel better. The Sox game was blaring on the radio, and I took a stool at the bar between a couple of the regulars, an empty seat on either side of me. Tim must have seen me comin'. He grumbled "Bobber" by way of greeting and plopped a tall glass of Pabst in front of me. Tim seemed to wear the same mustard-stained shirt every day, and it stretched over his gut and under his gray apron. On the back of his big noggin perched a chewed up straw boater – a relic from the nineties.

"Any score yet?" I asked.

Tim didn't seem to feel the question worthy of response, but Little Phil to my right (he was as shrunken as a human can get, the oldest guy in Canaryville) said, "No score. Bottom of the first." His voice had squeaked out, seemingly disembodied, from under his over-sized snap-brim.

I took my beer in hand and spun around on the stool, leaning my elbows back on the bar, so I wouldn't feel all hunched over. In forty years, I didn't fancy having Little Phil's posture.

At the back of the room, in its darkest corner, sat Mickey at his usual table, his bookie's paperwork stacked in semi-orderly piles around him. We made eye contact and he motioned me towards him with a look that said he had business to discuss. I knew I didn't owe him any money – I rarely bet – so my Pabst and I got off our stool and wandered over to him without fear. I wouldn't say we were best friends exactly, but we were old schoolyard chums. As boys, I'd won many marbles off him and it must have always stuck in his craw, because he often brought up the subject.

"Well, as I live and breathe – Bobber Maxwell, himself," Mickey said. "A celebrity in our humble tavern today. Have a seat, Bobber."

"Shut up, Mickey," I said, pulling up a chair and sitting, "you just saw me in here yesterday."

"Hey, you gonna let me win back some of my mibs?"

"Any time, Mickey. They're still in a sock on the top shelf of my closet."

"Pewie! You put my marbles in one of your smelly socks? Thanks a lot, pal." This was an old routine between us. But now it was over.

"So how ya fixed for blades, Mickey? What's the good word?"

"Oh, you know," he said, indicating the pile of scribbled on scraps of paper in front of him, "the ole crapola." He always wore the same felt hat, with a stain of sweat where the band had once been. He removed the hat now revealing his sweat plastered blonde locks. He wiped his wet forehead on his shirtsleeve and replaced the hat. "So, how about you? Workin' anywhere yet? Someone told me you might be joinin' the force."

I chuckled. "The police? Yeah, I've thought about it. They tell me I might be too old to start that."

"Too old?" Mickey said, rolling his eyes, a demented leprechaun. "What shite. A big Mick like you? Famous boxer? Army guy? They'd be nuts to turn you down."

"Well, I still might – "

"Look, if yer lookin' to pick up a little change," he said, getting down to brass tacks, "I might have some work for ya." He flashed his yellowy grin at me like Mr. Opportunity.

"I've told ya before, Mickey, I don't fancy myself the enforcer type." He'd asked me to break an arm or two for him in the past, but I had no appetite for putting the hurt on some poor family guy with a gambling problem. The idea made me shudder.

"Look, Bobber, I got this guy, Chauncey – a real compulsive. He's into me for a gee. And now he's avoiding me. A message has to be sent."

"Well, let someone else be the telegraph boy," I said, getting up. "You shouldn't let those poor clowns run up such big tabs with you."

"Hey, I'm a business man. This is a business like any other business. I'll give ya ten percent of anything yer collect off 'im. Just cuz we go back so far. That's a possible hunert smackers, Bobber."

"I'm leaving before I'm tempted. See ya in the marble ring, Mickey."

We both chuckled and my Pabst and I sidled away through the smoky air.

There had been a certain night, about ten years ago, when I had entered this place and been applauded by the crush of patrons. They had all come to listen to my first fight that had been broadcast on the radio. I had won gloriously against Pillar Palmer with a K.O. in the fifth. And the crowd at Tim's had all waited more than two hours for me to finally show up from downtown. And when I had come through that door I'd been a hero. Canaryville's hero. Their hero. Nothing had felt so good in all my life. And everyone wanted to buy me a beer.

No one had bought me any beers lately. It was understandable. But I certainly did not care much for the idea of walking through this same door and have everyone fear me – wondering whose leg I might have just gotten done busting. No. Better to be a former hero no one bought beers.

I sat back on my perch, facing away from the bar.

"Did ya hear that homer?" Little Phil asked.

"Yeah," I lied. "It was great."

"It was a Yankee homer, not for the Sox, you jerk."

"Sorry, Phil, I didn't really hear it."

"Asshole." And I recalled in that moment that Little Phil had been one of the guys who had bought me a beer that night a decade ago.

I shut up for awhile and nursed my Pabst, trying to focus on the game for real and only having partial success.

Tim's was filling up, people were drifting in after work as the ball game dragged on – it was not exactly a nail-biter.

Three young women sat huddled at a table by the front window, smoking and talking. I recognized Peggy O'Kief with two friends. She wasn't crying exactly, but the pale white skin of her face seemed a bit puffy around the eyes and her mouth was drawn in a tight thin-lipped line. Her two friends seemed equally serious, and I could tell they must be talking about her sister Erin. I didn't really want to walk over there, but my dumb old legs had other ideas.

The three young women stopped talking as I reached their table.

"Ladies. Peggy, Maxine, Sheila."

"Oh, Bobber, hi," they said, loosely in unison. They weren't unhappy to see me, but I wasn't being greeted with open arms either.

"Sorry to intrude on your conversation."

"Haven't seen yer for awhile, Bobber," said Peggy. She took a last drag from the cigarette she had going and stubbed out the butt in the overflowing ashtray.

"Hey, listen, Peggy," I said, suddenly really wishing my legs had minded their own damn business, "your parents were over at our place today…"

"Yeah?" Peggy asked, clearly not wanting to commit to knowing what I was going to say until I said it.

"Yeah. I just wanted to say I'm sorry about Erin. I hope she turns up." It sounded like such a lousy, lunk-headed thing to say, but I had said it.

"So they told you all about it?"

"Yeah. They were just hoping some neighbor had information about her. Sadly we didn't. But Ma and I were sure upset to hear about it."

"I love your mother," said Peggy. Her two friends shook their heads in agreement.

"Henrietta is the best," said Maxine.

Tears formed in Peggy's eyes. They flowed down her cheeks. She bent over the table and her friends leaned in with tissue and attentive cooing – while I stood there like a numb nuts.

"I'm so sorry, Peg," I finally said. "It must be horrible. I mean it is horrible." I mercifully was able to make myself shut up then.

"It is," Peggy said, looking up at me with a grim smile – but by doing so, letting me off the hook so I didn't feel like a total ass. "It's quite horrible."

"And you don't know where she was livin' except somewhere in the North Loop."

"She said she could see that Tribune Tower real well from her new place. That's all I know."

"This guy she was seeing," I stammered. "Vaughn, what?"

"Picout. Vaughn Picout. They even told yer about him, huh?"

Now I felt almost certain I'd heard that name. Maybe something to do with one of my fights? I just couldn't grasp it.

"Yeah. Yer dad wants to kill him. I understand why. Won't answer his phone, huh?"

29

"No. I met him once, you know. Erin brought him to lunch with us one day – this was just before she moved out."

"So she was going with him before she moved out of your parents'?"

"Yeah." Peggy had her tears under control now. "A total creep. Afterwards I asked Erin what she saw in him, but she just got defensive, so I let it go."

"And you think he was behind her move?"

"I really do."

"Hey, do you have his number on you? Can I have it?"

"Yeah," said Peggy. "You gonna call it?"

"Sure," I said, "I think I want to. I might make some other calls for you guys. I don't know – I still know some people downtown. You never can tell."

Peggy dug through her purse, pulled out a matchbook that had a number scrawled on the back in ink. She then produced an eyebrow pencil and copied the number onto one of Tim's paper napkins. She handed the napkin to me and I stuck it into my inside jacket pocket.

"Thanks. Like I said, you never can tell."

"Well, I appreciate this," said Peggy. "I doubt you'll have any better luck, but it can't hurt. Let us know if the creep answers."

"What exactly did ya find creepy about the guy?" I asked.

"Oh, you know, some people just hit yer the wrong way. He wore what looked like a bowling shirt to lunch with two ladies. No class. Mostly he just seemed evasive. Never looked you in the eye when he was talkin' to ya, that kinda thing. Hair in place but way too oily. A real Oily Boyd. Erin never cared for those Oily Boyd types. Weird."

"Bowling shirt?" I asked.

"Yeah. Well, it looked like one to me, anyway. It didn't have his name writ on it, or any writing at all. Just shortsleeve and shiny – broad horizontal stripes. Also reminded me of a carnival worker. Just not the kind of shirt normal people wear in public." She shook her head. I knew her friends would have liked to giggle at her description, but they didn't dare. "A creep."

I told Peggy I'd call her in a day or two just to touch base, and I left them to resume their conversation.

Back at the bar, I drained my beer, left some coins where Tim would see them, and I got the hell out of there. The Sox weren't going to hold my attention this day.

On the way home, I saw Pete Hoolihan's plumbing van driving towards me. Oh, brother, I thought. But the van only slowed slightly as it passed, and Pete gave me a cheerful little wave as it did. And then it was gone – headed for South Bend I presumed. Suddenly, I didn't see how I could ever bear to be with Maeve ever again. Whatever was going on between her and Pete (or, more likely, just with Maeve) it would have to resolve itself without any further involvement from me.

Back at the house, I went up to my room, put on a necktie, traded my windbreaker for a sports coat (transferring the napkin Peggy had given me), plopped on one of Pa's old fedora's I'd been using (I needed to buy a new one for myself – just one more thing I hadn't gotten around to yet) and went back downstairs.

The keys to the old DeSoto were still hanging on a hook next to the backdoor. We used the car so little the keys had started to become invisible to me – I was glad to discover Ma had not moved them. Now I took them and headed outside.

Ma was hanging a fresh load of wash, a couple clothespins in her mouth. She looked at me strangely when she saw me in the hat and tie – my look had become abnormally casual lately and I often went around without either.

"Where the hell do you tink yer goin'," she grunted, the clothespins clenched in her teeth, "dressed like half a human bean all of a sudden?"

"I feel restless, Ma. Thought I'd take the car out for a spin." I jingled the keys in front of her. "Blow the dust off."

She took the clothespins out of her mouth and said with some suspicion, "You talkin' about you or the DeSoto?"

"Both, I guess. I won't be home for supper, think I'll head into town. Can I bring you back anything, from the market or anywhere?"

"No, just don't go crackin' up. Hey, I don't even know if there's gasoline in dat bloody ting."

"If there isn't, I'll get some. I'm more worried about the battery. Don't wait up."

"They want ya ta have a license ta drive around in dem tings now, ya know."

"I got a license – courtesy of Uncle Sam. I left a Jeep double-parked in Berlin, but, don't worry, the Burgermeister waived that fine!"

Her eyes were definitely burning a hole in my back, but I did not turn around. I went through the back gate and around to the garage door that opened onto the alley.

I swung open both halves of the garage door, and there was the DeSoto, soaking up the daylight for the first time in months. A little dusty looking but pretty much the way it looked when Pa brought it home. It wasn't so much he had taken great care of it (even though he had), it was just that he had passed away only a couple of months after buying it. There had been no payments for Ma and I to make – he had bought it with cash, money he had saved for his retirement. A little gift for himself to drive to the ballgame in rather than take the bus. And wherever else he had planned to take it; we never really found out.

She was a beauty, though. Surely getting to be some kind of antique by now – time had surely passed her by – but still drivable. I had had her out briefly after my discharge. I was worried about that battery though.

I got into the four door yellow beauty and turned the ignition. With much moaning (and jiggling the clutch on my part) the engine roared to life. I eased into the alley, got out and swung the garage doors shut, and I was off. I caught Jerry still messing around at his Texaco station, and he gave her a quick once over. There was plenty of gas. He thought he knew where to order me a new set of tires (these weren't readily available – no emergency, but I'd want them soon), and he did recommend a new battery and a lube job in the not so distant future. But I was safe for a drive into town tonight. After refusing his offer to buy her, I headed north, looking to hook up with Archer Avenue.

There was still plenty of daylight left, but I didn't expect to be coming home till well after dark.

After finding Archer, I stayed with it a little while till I turned north onto State Street. I headed for the Loop.

It was unclear to me how those private dicks would go about it, but I wanted to see if I might not be able to have a little chat with Vaughn Picout.

# Chapter Two

I got a couple odd looks from fellow motorists and pedestrians alike, but the DeSoto handled well enough and blended into normal traffic. The clutch was a bit temperamental, I didn't see how a person could get used to it, but I managed fine.

The traffic on State got a little more stop and go as I got nearer the Loop. But it was, after all, a work day and this was the rush hour. I pressed on, the buildings of downtown now surrounding me. I headed the DeSoto right on Monroe for a couple blocks then took a left onto Michigan Avenue.

Soon, the Tribune Tower hove into view. My plan was to get as close to it as I could, find somewhere to park, get out and nose around, see what I could see. If nothing came of this lovely strategy, I would just drive home and try to think of something else to do. But that was the key phrase. I wanted "to do" something for the O'Kiefs. I knew them. I knew Erin – she was a decent kid. Never mind how Colin may have approached the police – I thought what they had told him was horrible. Maybe they were within the letter of the law in what they said. But there were gray areas. And people knew when family members had gone missing and when they hadn't. And maybe Erin was alive and fine someplace. But maybe if people waited too long to locate her, that status might soon change for the worse.

I drove over the Chicago River and passed the Tribune Tower on my right. There were no parking spots available on Michigan Avenue, so I went up to the next street and turned left. A couple blocks in there were plenty of open spots. I picked a likely place and parked.

The spot I had chosen was directly in front of a drugstore called Millie's Soda Fountain.

I got out of the car and locked up. Then I opened the heavy front foor of Millie's and made the little bell tinkle. The soda clerk/waitress stood idly nursing a cigarette down at the far end of the counter, but when I entered she stubbed out her smoke and strolled over.

I sat down on a stool near the door and ordered a cup of coffee and a hamburger. The waitress (a pretty sandy-haired kid in her early twenties), dressed in the standard black and white uniform with hairnet, poured my coffee then went in back to cook my burger. There was a tall, puffy pharmacist still on duty in the back of the store, but he and the waitress seemed the only employees in the place.

As I sipped my coffee and waited for my food, I got out the phone number Peggy O'Kief had copied for me on the napkin. The eyebrow pencil had smudged a bit when I had transferred the napkin from my windbreaker to my sports coat, but it was still readable.

There were a couple of dark wooden phone booths near the front door, so I decided to take my first baby step in this endeavor. I entered the nearest booth, put in my dime, and dialed.

It rang and rang. And rang and rang some more. I saw the waitress come out with my hamburger, so I gave up. I sat back down, and the burger smelled great. There were also some golden brown French fries next to the sandwich. The young woman was refreshing my coffee, and she said, "You didn't ask for them, but we had some fries left over in the fryer, so I gave you some free of charge. Um, hope you don't mind."

"Oh, heck no," I said, "they look terrific. I'll eat 'em. I'm starved. Thanks!"

"No problem. Let me know if you need anything else. I should probably get back to work straightening the newsstand." She glanced guiltily in the direction of the druggist. "I'll be over there straightening the magazines."

On impulse, I said, "Listen… I'm from down on the South Side. I'm up here tryin' to get in touch with an old neighbor of mine who's supposed to live around here. Her name is Erin O'Kief. You wouldn't know her, would you?"

The girl thought carefully and said, "No. I don't know anyone with that name. I've known a couple Erins, I mean, but not your neighbor. Don't have an address?"

"Just that she lives in the north Loop someplace. Not very specific, I know."

"No," she chuckled. "There are a lot of places to live around here."

"I guess so. Hey, you wouldn't know her boyfriend, would you? She's supposed to be dating a fella named Vaughn Picout. Ring a bell?"

She looked thoughtful again, then said. "Naw, not really. But," and she paused oddly, "that name sounds a little familiar though." So she thought it was familiar too. Maybe it was just because "Vaughn Picout" was an unusual name. "I'm sure I don't know the guy, but it seems like I've heard the name somewhere. Huh."

"Well," I said, handing her my phone number I had scribbled down on my own napkin, "if you think of where you heard of him before give me a call willya, please. If I'm not there, just leave a message with my Ma – we live down in Canaryville. My name is Bobber Maxwell, I wrote it down there."

"Bobber Maxwell?" she asked suddenly coming to life. "You're not that boxer guy, are ya?"

"Yeah, um, one and the same. You ever see me fight or something?"

She giggled. "Oh, no. No. I'm not a boxing fan or nothin' like that. I just know your name from the papers – and the radio."

"Yep. My name has been in those things all right."

"Well, nice to meet you, Mr. Maxwell, my name is Birdie – short for Roberta. Like I said, I'll be over there if you need anything else." She ripped off a green tab from her pad, slapped it in front of me, and went over to the newsstand.

I went to town on the burger and fries. They were greasy, but very flavorful. I had gotten pretty hungry.

I opened my wallet, and thought better of it. I had a decent amount of cash on me, but I was really trying to make that last as long as possible. I decided to pay my tab with leftover change from Tim's. Digging into my pants pocket, I fished out enough to pay for my meal (and to leave Birdie a decent tip), when she wandered back in front of me, holding a folded newspaper.

"Here. I guess you'd want to read this. I knew I'd heard that name."

She handed me the paper, the front section of the Chicago American, folded back to show page five. The Police Blotter. Birdie had circled a tiny article which sat next to an ad for a used car dealership.

The tiny headline read: BODY FOUND IN LAKE NEAR NAVY PIER. The deceased had been identified as one Vaughn Picout, 31, of Chicago. The police suspected foul play because of "unspecified" wounds on the victim's body. They asked for any information anyone might have. Picout's exact address was not given. However, it did say his wallet had been on his person, still with cash in it, so robbery did not appear to be the motive. The police wanted to speak to anyone who had known Picout..

"Jesus Christ," I said involuntarily, setting the paper down on the counter. The words in the blurb had hit me like a ton of bricks. I tried not to let it show, but I was really shaken up. There hadn't been any mention of Erin, of course, but it couldn't be good news for her either. Clearly the O'Kief family had not gotten wind of this article yet, and I could only imagine what their reaction would be when they did.

That name "Vaughn Picout" suddenly rang with a bit more clarity. Maybe it was only a false memory, but I could have sworn that was the name of one of the sparring partners my old gym had once arranged for me. If I were right, I think I had gotten in the ring with the guy for only one session.

"Can I keep this?" I asked.

"Sure," said Birdie. "That was where I had seen that name – I read it there. So, you think that's the guy your neighbor was dating?"

"Yeah. I'm afraid so. How many people could have a name like that?"

"Gee," Birdie said, very apprehensively, "I – I hope your friend is all right."

"Christ, I hope so. I mean, this is a real shocker. Excuse me, Birdie, I think I need to use the telephone again."

"Sure thing," said Birdie, clearly upset because she had brought me bad news in an attempt to be helpful.

Stepping back into the phone booth, I decided it wouldn't hurt to give Cully's Gym a call. The coin slot got fed. I still remembered the number, and, as I dialed, I felt a pang of guilt that I had not stopped by since my discharge. Maybe I should start working out again.

I heard the line ringing. After a few, someone picked up. There was a great roaring echo of human voices shouting, punching bags getting punched, etcetera.

"Yeah?" growled a familiar voice. "Cully's Gym."

"Hey, Tonsils, is that you?" I asked.

"That's right," said Tonsils, "who's this? I can't hear for shit in here!"

"It's Bobber!"

"Hey, Bobber, how the fuck are ya?" yelled Tonsils. The story of his nickname went something like: as a little child so long ago – Tonsils was now easily in his mid-seventies – he had accidentally swallowed iodine. He had survived but the poison had scarred his larynx. So he grew up with a voice like nuts and bolts rattling around in a tin can. His parents never grasped what a "larynx" was supposed to be, so he just became known as "Tonsils." The last decade or so he had run Cully Benson's gym for him. Cully was even older than Tonsils and had moved to Florida years ago.

"I'm great, Tonsils, great. Back from the war and all that."

"Yeah, all that," said Tonsils.

"I won't keep you. I just wanted to ask – is there a guy named Vaughn Picout who works out there? He's a member, isn't he?"

There was a brief pause, and Tonsils answered, "Sure, I know that greasy cocksucker. He your buddy? He hasn't been in for awhile. His membership may have expired."

"No, not my buddy. I just have a letter for him. Some guy I met in the army knew Vaughn, knew I was also from Chicago, and asked me to take it to him," I fibbed. Tonsils didn't seem to know old Vaughn had been murdered, and I didn't feel like it was a smart thing to tell him this news through the distracting circumstances of this phone conversation. And I sure didn't want to mention Erin. "You wouldn't be able to look up his address for me, would you?  So I can send the message to him?"

"Look up his address?" asked Tonsils with annoyed hesitation in his rattling voice.  "Jesus, Bobber.  You know I can't do that.  Do you know what old Cully would do to me if he knew I was givin' away private member information like that?  Even a former member?  He'd have my nuts in a bag!"

Old Cully had been a twisted little broomstick of a man the last time I'd laid eyes on him, and it was hard to imagine him being a threat to anyone's nuts, including those of Tonsils.  Still, I had to respect Tonsils wanting to uphold the policies of his boss.  I was a little pissed that I didn't rate a bending of the rules.  Then again, I hadn't been back there since Pearl Harbor.

"I just thought…"

"Tell you what," said Tonsils, "you send your letter here and we can forward it to the greasy cocksucker."

"Thanks, I might just do that," I said.

"Listen, I gotta go.  Don't be a stranger, Bobber."

"I won't.  Take it easy, Tonsils."

And he hung up.

God damn. I had come so close. I could just see that beaten-to-death shoebox (stuffed with index cards containing members' stats) sitting on the corner of the desk in the gym office. Maybe a visit to my old gym was in order.

No, I certainly would not be a stranger.

Back at the counter, I made sure Birdie got her tip. "You've been a serious help to me."

"Yeah?"

"I think I may have tracked down an address. I really appreciate it." And I headed for the door.

"I hope you find your friend!" Birdie said. I hope so too, I thought.

I thanked her again, with a reminder to call if she heard anything else, and left Millie's.

As I got back into the DeSoto, I realized the breeze off Lake Michigan had put a chill in the air. The sun had not yet set, but the summer-like day was gone. I would have preferred to stay back at the soda fountain and have cute little Birdie endlessly refill my coffee. But, alas, other tasks were summoning.

I tore the police blotter blurb from the page Birdie had given me, sticking the item into my inside coat pocket.

Cully's was not terribly far away, just a few blocks north on Huron. I put the car in gear and left the comfort of my parking space.

The decade before the war, Cully's had been like a second home to me. They had really cared about my boxing career, Cully and Tonsils acting as my de facto managers so much so that I never signed a real one. In fact, maybe if I"d gone into the Chicago Boxing Commission's office with Tonsils at my side, when I first got home, maybe things would have gone better. Maybe I'd still have a career left to salvage because Tonsils did not suffer fools and would not have put up with their shit. But instead, I'd gone in alone and listened to their crap about me being "too old." And I'd quietly accepted it. Consequently, I had left the offices bitter. For some unexplainable reason, it had not even occurred to me to stop off and visit Cully's Gym first.

I couldn't blame Tonsils for putting the screws to my conscience.

Getting back onto Michigan Avenue, I made the turn north, and, within just a few minutes, I was making the turn onto Huron. In even less time, I was pulling into Cully's small parking lot, a glorified strip of gravel that hugged the west side of the building.

Getting out of the car and walking around to the front door, I realized it had been years since I had done it. But this little ritual stroll had been such a part of my life it felt as if I'd only done it yesterday. Cully's Gym was housed in a low, squat building. One story only, with a matching basement. The ground floor held the open gym, exercise equipment, two full boxing rings, and the offices; the basement contained the steam cabinets, lockers and showers, rubdown and storage rooms.

Through the glass doors I could see the usual ground floor activity, bags being punched, etcetera. I entered.

Nobody took any notice of me, so I wandered into the noise and the ever-present pungency – a combination of old leather, human sweat, and witch hazel.

The place was fairly busy, the usual weekday late afternoon crowd. I stood by a clump of disheveled folding chairs and scanned the faces. Funny, once I would have recognized just about everybody in the place. Now, I didn't recognize anyone.

At first, there was no sign of Tonsils. I looked over at the office door behind the front counter. The door hung wide open, as usual, but it was dark in there, and no one was manning the counter either.

First I heard him. Then I saw him coming up the stairs from the basement. He was chewing the hell out of some kid in sweat clothes who trailed after with a medicine ball clutched against his chest.

Tonsils hadn't changed at all. He was a terrifying scarecrow come to life, taller than me, with skin the color and texture of a greasy paper bag. Under ordinary circumstances, I would have walked right up to him. But a weird shyness had come over me just like the first day I had met him.

Since I was standing off by myself in street clothes, he spotted me right away. He finished with the kid, an employee of the gym, and motioned me over. The kid escaped the vicinity of his boss with comical speed.

No time for shyness now.

"I was nearby so I thought I would stop, after all," I said, shaking Tonsils' hand. He gripped me firmly, but there was wariness in his manner.

"So, you bring that letter thing?" he asked.

"No, no, that's back at the house in Canaryville with Ma. I'll bring it round some other time."

"Ah, that mudder of yours is somethin' else."

"That she is. No, I thought I'd check out the old joint, renew my membership, if that's okay."

Finally, I'd said something that got half a smile out of him. "Oh, sure, Bobber, we can do that. Let's go into the office." He walked behind the counter and I followed.

He flipped on the light and it was like walking back in time. The room wasn't exactly huge, but it was decent-sized for an office. It just seemed tiny because of all the crap crammed into it. In the middle sat the desk and a couple chairs. Every wall had at least a couple, or more, filing cabinets of varying size and age – each with one or more drawers pulled partially open. Every inch of wall surface had something covering it, from framed photographs to yellowed newspaper clippings held on with yellowed and curled strips of cellophane tape. The light in the room came from a bare bulb which swung from a stained ceiling tile by a frayed black cord. There were papers and shit stacked haphazardly onto every horizontal surface.

The office hadn't changed at all, either.

Tonsils plopped into the desk chair and I moved a stack of manila envelopes onto the floor so I could take the interviewee seat. Tonsils had left the door open, but the gym noise was reduced enough in here so you could have a conversation in a more normal volume.

"So, Bobber, you gettin' back in the ring?" He said it more as a statement than as a question, as if to imply that, of course, that's why I was here. It stung to hear it. I wasn't at all sure how to answer.

"I don't know, maybe. Mostly I thought I'd just get into shape for starts."

"We can get you a card right away. Maybe no more than a couple months. Weren't you fighting exhibitions all during the war?"

"Ha, ah, no, I did a couple of those here in the states before I shipped out. But once I was in Europe, all that was forgotten. All soldier boy stuff."

Yeah, soldier boy stuff. The full story of those exhibition fights went like this: freshly arrived at basic training in dear old Camp McCoy, I wasted no time in letting my sergeant know I was a big deal in the world of Chicago boxing. I told myself I wanted to keep my boxing skills honed

51

during this hitch, but I'm sure my motivations were really ego-driven. Instead of telling me to fuck off, Sgt. Mullins seemed interested. I guess they were always looking for diversions. The next day, I was approached by a real wheeler-dealer named Sgt. Chambers. This bird filled my head with all kinds of talk about my touring the states, from camp to camp, with a big boxing exhibition. Chambers put together two bouts right there in the Camp McCoy gym. The first one was an embarrassment with me going up against three wobbly-kneed sparring partners, where it felt like I was teaching a class in boxing. This bout was poorly attended and not very "paid attention to." But the bout Chambers put together for the following week was a roaring success. He'd managed to find another local boxing up-and-comer, one Gary Kent, a big farm boy from Council Bluffs, Iowa. Now my fellow basic trainees had something to yell about – and bet on. The place was packed. Gary was an inch taller than me and outweighed me by ten pounds. But I out-classed him, and he was too slow. I gave the whooping soldiers a good show; but in the seventh round I let Gary have it. I tried for a clean knock-out, but he was protecting his face too well. So I hammered at the side of his skull till he finally crumpled. In the end, those who bet against me acted like they hated me. And those who won money off me were, for the most part, indifferent. I never heard from Chambers again. I sent him a couple telegrams shortly after I left Camp McCoy, but they went unanswered. And before I knew it, I was in France trying not to get my ass shot off.

That was all there was to tell about my army boxing exhibitions except for this footnote. Shortly after VE Day, I was still in Germany, part of a crew in place to help restore some type of order to Berlin. It was dangerous work. Not all Germans were willing to accept our word that the war was over and that they had lost. Most were ready for peace – some still wanted to fight. Berlin itself, in many areas, was one horrible pile of bombed out buildings after another. I remember, it was a beautiful sunny day, but the air choked you with the stench of death. I walked around the remains of a hotel, and leaning against a pile of cinder block rubble was Gary Kent. I hadn't seen him since our fight back at Camp McCoy. And now he was dead. He stared with unseeing eyes, his left arm twisted bizarrely behind him as if he'd gotten his hand caught in the halftrack of a passing tank, and the shock had killed him. I shut the poor bastard's eyes and notified the guys on my team who took care of such things. His dog-tags confirmed his identity, still I was glad I could at least back them up with firsthand knowledge, for the sake of his family.

So, no, I didn't feel like going into all that with Tonsils.

"Well, that's a shame," he replied to the short version of my exhibition fights' tale. "But, ya had to beat those fuckin' Nazis."

"Yeah. But anyway, Tonsils, I have bigger obstacles to getting back in the ring. When I came home after discharge, the Boxing Commission wouldn't renew my license. Thought I was too old now."

Tonsils' eyes suddenly flashed with anger. "How old are you?"

"Gonna turn thirty-four next month."

"What horse shit. Who told you you were too old? That cocksucker Porter?"

I had to chuckle at Tonsils' talent for seeing through all the layers. "Yeah, he was the one who spoke to me. Good call."

"Oh, listen, there are ways around that mealy-mouth," said Tonsils. "Make no mistake, you're getting up there, but lots of guys older than you are still out there sluggin' in sanctioned matches. You let me go down there with you. I'll straighten his bloomers. But let's get you back on the books here. You got yer ten bucks?"

"Sure."

He rummaged through the drawers. It might cost me some cash I didn't want to part with (I was desperately clinging to the small amount I had squirreled away of that fifty dollars a month the army had paid me), but it seemed like a good idea. Truth be told, that meeting I'd had with Porter had kind of soured me on the idea of getting back in the ring at all. And the memory of Gary Kent wasn't helping. But I did belong here at Cully's, working out nearly every day like I had for the better part of my twenties, I knew that at least.

Right now, however, I had my eye on that dilapidated shoe box on the corner of the desk. There was no lid, and all the yellowed membership cards were visible.

"Gotta run downstairs and get me one of the government forms. Be right back."

Tonsils shot out of his chair and left the room. I did not hesitate. I turned the shoe box around and started flipping madly.

Tonsils' alphabetizing may have left something to be desired, but at least all the P's seemed to be lumped together. And there it was: PICOUT, VAUGHN!

I memorized the address on Hubbard, stuffed the card back into place, and spun the shoe box back around just in time to beat Tonsils as he exploded back into the office.

"Got it!" he said. "Gotta keep those Springfield cocksuckers happy."

So moments later, as I filled out a State of Illinois form, Tonsils had pulled the shoe box over to him and was fishing out my old membership record. I wondered if he could tell that someone had been going through the cards. But he showed no sign.

I finished the form. Then I took out the precious ten bucks from my wallet and handed it to him. He marked my card PAID and wrote the date. I saw that my last fee had been paid September of 1941. If I'd only known.

Tonsils put away my card, stuffing it in amongst the other M names, and shoved the shoe box back in place. He leaned back in his chair. "You bring yer workout clothes? You wanta put in some time on the bag right now?  I can even get you a sparring partner, if you like?"

"Oh, no, no," I said a little too sheepishly, "not tonight.  Nothing like that.  I'll bring some stuff for my locker next time.  I just came to re-up, you know."

"'Cause I'll go in there and face Porter and those other sons o' bitches with ya.  I'm sure we can get you in the ring again.  Don't lose no more sleep over it."

"That's great.  I think I'll take you up on that."  This was feeling awkward.  And I felt badly about how I had coldly cut him out of my life once I'd enlisted.  I never even said goodbye to him or anyone here at Cully's before I headed for boot camp.  Truth be told, Tonsils had been the closest thing I'd had for a father figure since Pa died.  Tonsils and Cully – but especially Tonsils – had really taken me under their wings.  And I'd behaved like an ungrateful little pissant.

Tonsils drew in his breath oddly and paused, staring a hole through me.  Finally he said, "So, did you find the address you were looking for in that box?"

I'd been set up.  Clearly, he'd been expecting me to do just what I had at my first opportunity.

Over his shoulder, hanging on the wall, I spotted a framed photo of me in the ring, the ref holding my hand up in victory, my mouthpiece dangling off my lower lip, my eyes glazed-over, my hair plastered in sweat against my forehead. A marvelous moment caught in black and white by some newspaper photog.

My face flushed red. I felt stupid and ashamed. There was nothing for it but to come clean, no matter how mortifying.

"Okay, listen, Tonsils. I want to apologize…"

So I told him, as quickly as possible, the whole story about my neighbor Erin going missing, how she'd been seeing Picout, how I'd just discovered that Picout had been murdered and how I feared that Erin had met the same fate only she hadn't yet been found. As I spoke, it felt amazingly easy, and I wondered at my denseness at not having gone with the truth in the first place.

I showed him the newspaper blurb Birdie had given me.

He whistled and handed it back. "Holy fuck. Murdered," he said. "Little prick probably had it coming. I didn't say so over the phone, just in case you two really were pals, but I once caught him going through unsecured lockers. So I booted his ass. He slunk away and we never saw him again."

"No, he was no pal of mine."

"You know you could have told me all this from the start. I would have given you the address if I'd had the facts."

"I realize that now, Tonsils. Again, I couldn't be sorrier."

"You should really go to the cops with this information."

"Oh, I intend to," I said. Then I told him about Erin's brother Colin, and how he'd ruffled the feathers of the police – all that stuff they'd said about adult women and their families. "I'll go to the cops just as soon as I try to find her myself, in case she's in imminent danger. Waiting for the police to act might only make things worse."

Tonsils looked at me dubiously, but I think he saw my point a little. Maybe. In any case, it was time for me to leave. I promised him I would be back for a workout in just a couple days.

His parting words were: "Take it easy, Kid. Don't get yerself killed." It was good advice.

I drove over to Hubbard. Picout's address ended up being only a few blocks from Millie's Soda Fountain.

There still seemed to be plenty of daylight left.

It did not take very long to find the exact building number. I was worried about just blindly making a beeline for it, in case the police, who surely also had learned the address, were watching the place. But there didn't seem to be any watchful presence. After a couple trips around the block, I found a parking spot down from the corner of the building.

It was one of those addresses stuck shoulder to shoulder with the buildings on either side of it. All the structures on this particular stretch of Hubbard seemed a bit shabby. The first floor was taken up with a dry cleaner's – which appeared to be "out-of-business" currently. The three floors above looked to be apartment units.

Directly next to the front door of the dry cleaner's was a matching door – and through the glass window of this door a long stairway could be seen leading up into darkness and the floors above.

I expected this door to be locked, but as I pulled on the knob, it swung open easily. The catch had been removed from the knob – probably long ago.

I stepped inside with as much confidence as I could muster. The door closed behind me with only a slight noise. The echo of a few voices drifted down the steps. Someone was cooking fish. A radio was playing Glen Miller somewhere up there – or maybe it was a phonograph. There was a bank of brass mailboxes at the foot of the stairs along the left wall. Scanning the boxes – some of which were unmarked – I found a pencil-scratched label showing a "V. Picout" as living in apartment Three-C.

So oily Vaughn had indeed been living here still at the time he'd gotten himself bumped off.

With this new information, I headed up the steps for the third floor.

At the second floor, I encountered no one. I took the next flight and reached the third. No one in the hall up here, either. It was very dark, and the open window at the end of the hall seemed to suck light out instead of the opposite. That music I'd heard was drifting down from up on the fourth floor. Murmuring voices seemed to come from all around me. Moving quickly, I found Apartment C.

I rapped on the door. I waited and rapped again. Glancing up and down the hall, it did not look like I was being observed by any curious neighbors, so I tried the knob. Locked.

There was no real plan in my mind, just flying by the seat of my pants. Stopping to think about it, I had gotten much farther than I imagined I would have on the drive into the city. I had discovered that the so-called "creep" Peggy O'Kief had met and disliked had somehow gotten himself murdered and dumped in the lake. And, most incredibly, I now found myself at the former threshold of said deceased creep. But now what? What was my next move?

Well, I answered myself, the only reason I was even here was to locate Erin O'Kief – to discover her relative safety. To bring her home if she was safe? Well, sure. That – if she were willing to go home. But now it looked as though she might even be implicated in Picout's murder. Had she murdered him? Maybe. I mean, it was possible, of course. I had no idea what the situation really was, what exactly Erin had gotten herself into.

One thing was sure – there was no more information to be had about Erin's whereabouts out here in this dim hallway. But there might be more information to be had about Erin on the inside of that apartment. Had I come all this way only to turn around and head back to Canaryville?

Of course not. The image of Peggy O'Kief crying down at Tim's flitted through my brain.

I was going to get into that apartment.

There had been several guys I'd known over the years who knew everything there was to know about picking locks. I was not among them, however. There was a guy in my platoon, in Europe, who had once tried to explain some of the basics to me. Right now, I wished I had paid more attention to him and not laughed at him and called him a burglar. Right now, in fact, I wished he was standing next to me.

I squatted down to get a better look at that lock. The first thing I noticed was that this door had the same kind of keyhole as our front door at home. Peeking into the keyhole, I could make out nothing but a very dark room. I dug my keys out of my pocket and tried both the front and backdoor keys of our house. Both froze in the lock, not budging one bit. I had a third smaller but similar key that was used for our cellar door. It didn't fit either, but with one big difference: it did not feel as frozen tightly in the lock. There was some slight give – I could wiggle it somewhat to the right and left.

I pulled the key out and looked at it. There was a new shiny spot on one of the edges. Not knowing what the hell I was doing, I stuck the key back in and turned it back and forth again, but this time bearing down hard to steer the key away from the side of the lock's interior that had been rubbing it shiny. I worked the key like this over and over for awhile, continuing to bear down on it this way, really giving it some elbow grease. And suddenly, the lock popped!

I removed the key and tried the knob. It opened easily in my grip. Glancing up and down the empty hall, I slipped inside the apartment and quietly shut the door behind me.

The air was hot and musky in there. A single window, covered in broken Venetian blinds, let in very little light – which now was looking pretty dusky out there anyway.

I felt with my hand along the wall till I found the double push buttons of the light switch. I pushed the protruding button, and light suddenly flooded the place.

It was a simple layout. There was a big main room with a table and a couple wooden chairs near that window. The room doubled as a bedroom – there was a double-sized unmade Murphy bed, pulled out from the wall, it's bed clothing twisted up and a mess. A couple of pillows from the Taft administration sat bunched up at its head. There was a nightstand and a chest of drawers. Two doors were in the wall opposite the bed. The open one looked to be a tiny bathroom. The closed door I took to be a clothes closet. Off in the right corner, next to the window, a tiny kitchenette had been inserted, complete with a little ice box and dangerously ancient hot plate. There were some socks and other clothing items scattered on the floor, along with some magazines and bits of paper.

The place reeked.

I decided to move about carefully and try to disturb as little as possible. I assumed the police had been here already but, frankly, there seemed no obvious evidence that they had. Maybe a couple cops had been let in by the building manager and then left after a couple glances around. In any case, I resolved to wipe with my hanky any surface I happened to touch.

As if walking on a carpet of baby chicks, I edged around the room. I opened the closed door and it did indeed prove to be a closet. Hanging inside were a couple men's shirts (and, yes, one looked like a bowling shirt) and a suit coat that had seen better days.

And there were several women's dresses and blouses (and, yes, they could have been worn by Erin). The top shelf held a beat up fedora and a couple women's hats. There were no extra shoes on the floor of the closet, but there were a couple closed cardboard boxes, the kind you get from the grocery store when you're going to move. These were sealed shut with masking tape. I decided to save snooping in these boxes till later. I moved to a dresser which stood between the closet and the bed.

The bureau was about chest high to me and had a long mirror attached to its top that needed re-silvering. I looked at my reflection in the imperfect surface. Maybe I was the creep – sneaking around like this. I avoided eye contact with myself. I needed a shave.

I gingerly opened the drawers. The ones devoted to men's clothing were a jumble of indifference. There was one filled with unmatched socks and a bottle half-filled with hair tonic. The drawers devoted to women's clothing were tidy and organized.

I respectfully lifted a pile of panties and there on the bottom of the drawer was a photograph. It was black and white, but even in gray tones you could just see all the little red heads. It was a group shot of the entire O'Kief clan taken at some Christmas gathering several years back. There were Erin and Peggy, probably in high school at the time.

Erin had been living here with Vaughn, at least for a while, that was certain. But where was she now? From the moldy sandwich on the edge of the sink, and the general mustiness of the air, it did not appear that anyone had been living in this apartment for several days.

Was Erin about to pop in through the door and ask me what the hell I was doing here? It didn't seem likely. A shiver ran through me thinking about that possibility she may have met the same fate as her boyfriend. I really wanted to believe she was still alive somewhere, but things weren't looking good.

On impulse, I took the photo and carefully eased it into my inside jacket pocket.

I wiped down all the handles and drawers I had touched so far and made everything look like it had.

Opening the ice box, I immediately shut it. Something very bad was going on in there. Holding my nose, I opened it once more for a better look. An open bottle of milk and a couple cartons of Chinese take-out did not seem like promising clues, so I shut the door again.

I took a peek in the tiny bathroom, hoping I wouldn't have to make use of it by puking up my poor, delicious Millie's Soda Fountain burger.

The room had no tub, only a mildewed shower stall complete with mildewed shower curtain. The floor in front of the shower was a snarl of twisted dirty towels. I gingerly poked a finger into the top towel – the surface felt dry as a bone. I nudged the snarl with my foot and a tiny cockroach – perhaps a teenager – came skittering out and made straight for a crack where the floor met the wall. No, it did not look like there had been any showers taken lately.

I was about to leave the room when I spied a page that had been torn from a magazine, and folded, leaning against the wall next to the toilet. Carefully picking it up with a piece of toilet paper, I shook it so gravity would help open it up. The page was a full length black and white photo of a snake – it had a light colored marking on its chin, and it was coiled and bearing some nasty-looking fangs. The caption at the bottom on the photo read: "Fer-de-lance." I didn't know what that meant. But I refolded the page carefully and wrapped the whole thing up in a couple layers of toilet paper. I slid it next to the photo of Erin's family.

Maybe, before new toilet paper could be purchased, the happy couple had been wiping themselves with glossy magazine pages. Or maybe it meant something more. At the moment, there was no way to tell. My instinct was to take it anyway. It felt right to follow my instincts. Maybe I was too old to join the police force – but maybe I might make a decent private investigator in my dotage.

If I didn't get myself shot and dumped in the lake first.

There were still those boxes in the closet to look through. And maybe those utensil drawers under the kitchen sink. I made a move towards the closet when there was some talking out in the hallway. I moved to the doorway and pressed the button to shut off the light, in case light could be seen under the door.

The voices got louder. Two guys walking down the hall making the floor boards squeak. They did not pause at the door of Three-C, however, and I heard them pass by and descend the stairs, still talking about a bus driver or something.

But my nerve was blown. Deciding that I had collected enough clues for one day, I opened the door (holding the knob with my hanky) and stepped out into the hall.

I shut the door behind me and pocketed my hanky. A minute or two crawled by where I tried to decide how best I might go about relocking the door – and whether it was even necessary to do so – when a voice spoke behind me.

It was a female voice.

"Oh, hello," said the voice. "Are you a friend of Vaughn?"

Keeping a cool head (or trying to), I turned around.

It was an attractive woman, older than me, maybe in her late thirties or early forties. Ironically, she was probably Maeve's age, but maybe a little older. She had blonde hair swept up on top of her head and dark eyebrows. Her frame was statuesque with an ample chest like a chorus girl, but she did not have the starved waistline of someone in show biz. She could have been a former chorus girl, now leading a normal life. At least as normal as you could get living in a dump like this.

Playing it cool, cool, cool, I said, "I only met Vaughn once years and years ago. I'm a friend of Erin O'Kief's. A former neighbor of hers." (Then I decided to add just a bit of an embellishment to my story, to make my being here in this hallway seem just a bit more reasonable; I hoped this lady hadn't seen me come out of the apartment.) "I told her parents I was coming into the city today and they asked if I could look her up – see if she needs anything."

"Oh, Erin," said the woman. "Oh, dear. So you don't know?"

"About what?" I fibbed. I didn't want this person to think – if I could help it – that I had anything to do with Picout's death."

The woman's expression darkened. "Vaughn, well. Vaughn has been killed." And after I put on a little show of being shocked, and then urgently asking about Erin, the woman said, "I'm Lana."

"Hi. I'm Bobber. Dumb nickname, but there it is."

"Huh. Okay, Bobber, nice to meet you. Look, I was just going to go 'round the corner for a bite to eat. Care to join me? I can tell you everything I know better on a full stomach."

"Okay, sure," I said, leaving out the part about already having eaten. I really needed to hear what this woman had to say about this subject.

"Then let me get my things, and I'll lead the way.

She got her things. And she led the way.

We ended up at a sooty little café a couple streets down. I did not point out my car, nor offer to drive. It was a nice night. We really didn't speak much on the way over except when she pointed out the place.

And said place was a long, thin building much like Millie's Soda Fountain had been. The only sign out front was a flickering neon dinosaur that said simply: FOOD. It wasn't packed but it was doing a fairly brisk business for supper. My wristwatch was back at home, but the clock on the wall behind the counter said it was going on seven in the evening. It was nearly dark out.

Lana led me all the way to the back and we took one of the empty booths. A teenage girl with black bangs brought us coffee and took our order.

Lana ordered a tuna sandwich and fries. I asked for another burger – and this time I also asked for fries. The truth be told, I can always eat. I have what you call a "high metabolism."

We were finishing up the food on our plates, the waitress having just refilled our coffees, when I broke the silence.

"So, um, Lana," I said, "what's all this about Vaughn being killed? Do you know where Erin is right now?"

She looked at me gravely and said, "I do not know where Erin is at the moment. It upsets me too because she and I seemed to be becoming pretty good friends. As for Vaughn, I barely ever spoke to him. But, like I said, it looks like he's been murdered."

"And how did you find this out?"

"Well, I first heard about it day before yesterday. Mr. Talarico who lives on the floor below me – he saw me at the mailboxes that evening, and he said, 'so ya hear? That Vaughn on your floor – he got hisself killed.' It was in the paper that night. A little article. Said he'd been shot and dumped in the lake." She must have read about Picout in a different paper. The American blurb I had said nothing about his being shot.

I continued to play dumb. "Did it say anything about Erin? Have you seen anything of her since you heard about Vaughn?"

"I haven't seen her at all for at least a week," she said. "I'm just waitin' for the cops to show up – to questions the neighbors, ya know?" She took out a cigarette case decorated with some kind of fancy lettering and designs. She offered me one and I declined with a wave of my hand and a sheepish grin. "You don't smoke?" she asked, lighting up with a lighter that appeared to match the case.

"I did for a while – in my teens and twenties. I just played around with them, though, just for image. But during the war – well, I saw too many guys despairing for them in those foxholes. When they were in short supply. Awful comfort in all that freezing mud. I got back and I couldn't touch them anymore. But go ahead, I don't mind if other people smoke."

She looked at me weirdly and took a huge drag on her cigarette. "Sounds simply hideous." She blew out a huge cloud aimed at the people in the booth across the aisle.

"Anyway," I said, "Do you think you should go to the police and tell them you know the murder victim's girlfriend?"

"Girlfriend," she muttered. "You do know she and Vaughn were shackin' up over there, right?" I just shrugged noncommittally as if it didn't matter to me one way or the other. "Well, I don't know. I'm kinda waiting to see if they do approach me. See, Erin would never come clean with me about her job – I think she and Vaughn worked at the same place. Weird people would come up to their place all the time. Sometimes in the middle of the night."

"How do you mean 'weird' people. How weird were they?"

She thought about that a couple seconds then said, "Carnival types, I guess. Men and women. I got the idea they worked for a magician or something. Anyway, I'm a little scared that they might think she was the one who killed Vaughn. Don't want to get Erin in any trouble unnecessarily."

"I see what you mean. No, of course not." I let that whole thing about working for a magician slide. But I intended to get back to it.

"Look, don't run off," said Lana, "I won't be gone long. Just gonna powder my nose."

She slid out of the booth and headed up the aisle towards the bathrooms.

I sat and sipped my coffee.

After a few minutes, a guy about my age, black hair and very skinny (about half my size), came up to me a bit sheepishly and said, "Excuse me, sir. Haven't I seen you box? You're that Bobber guy. Bobber Mansfield, right?"

"It's Bobber Maxwell. Right."

"Bobber Maxwell," he repeated, a bit embarrassed, "I was close. But I seen ya! I seen ya knock a guy out! Ah, which one was it?"

"I don't know," I tried to help, getting embarrassed a little myself. "Where was the fight you saw?"

"Where was it?" he asked himself, running his hand through his hair. "Maybe it was at the Medinah Temple."

"Yeah, I fought there on a couple cards. Was it Remo Schultz? I knocked him out at the Medinah."

"Naw, not that guy. Wish I had – I'd like to see you knock out a fuckin' kraut." Then his face lit up. "Hey, if I go get a piece of paper, can I have an autograph?  I mean, I don't mean to bother you – I could see you were having dinner with the lady."  He tried to wink at me conspiratorially, but it somehow fell apart in his eyelids.  He chuckled, embarrassed.

"Yeah, sure.  If you want it, I'll sign something for you."

"Ah, thanks," he said, "I'll be right back."

Shortly after he left, Lana returned from powdering her nose.

I could tell she was going to ask about the guy – when he returned with a handbill for a church picnic and a fountain pen.  He turned the handbill over so its blank side faced up, slapped it on the table next to my coffee , and he handed me the pen.

"Pardon me, lady.  Could ya make it to 'Blaine?'"

I took the pen and wrote, "To Blaine – Bobber Maxwell."  I blew on the ink a little, no blotter being available, and handed it back to Blaine.  You would have thought I'd handed him a check for ten grand.  He looked at it and grinned crazily.

"Aw, Jesus Christ, thanks so much, Mr. Maxwell. Pleased to meetcha! Bye, lady!" And Blaine scampered back up the aisle.

"Well, what was that all about?" Lana asked, lighting another smoke. "You famous or something?

So, as briefly as possible, I tried to fill in this non-boxing fan about my meteoric career in the ring. I included an explanation of my nickname, too.

"When I first started boxing in high school, I showed a great talent for evasion. The whole bobbing and weaving stuff – in order not to get punched. I only got better at it. No one has barely laid a glove on me. Well, there was this one time. But, trust me, that was a quality connection." I rubbed my jaw, remembering Orangutan's infamous punch yet again. "It hurts to get punched. That's why I also got so good at avoiding it."

I explained, too, why I was not currently working as a prizefighter.

Lana stared at me with fresh interest and said lightly, "So, if I ever need to have someone beaten up, I guess you're the guy to contact."

"Yeah, well, we'll see what I can do. Depends."

When she saw I was not going to join in on the humor of the idea, she dropped it. Changing the subject, she said, "If I buy your supper, would you consider walking me back to my apartment? I don't know if I'm going to make you late for whatever it is you originally came into the city for. But all this talk about murder and beating people up has made me a little nervous. It's dark out there now."

I confessed to her that finding Erin had really been my sole purpose for coming downtown.

"I'd be happy to walk you home, though. But let me pay this time. I ain't so broke that I can't buy you a tuna sandwich."

So I did pay our waitress for the whole ticket, and we left the place. I looked around for Blaine, but he wasn't there. I imagined him somewhere showing off his prize to his buddies. I never really understood the appeal of autographs myself, but if a person liked to collect them and they got a kick out of it – well, it certainly was more innocent than the hobbies of some people.

Even though there was still a steady stream of headlamps up and down Hubbard (there are always cars on the streets of Chicago, no matter what the hour – I imagine it's the same in any big city), traffic had definitely slowed. I was used to the smell of the city, but this neighborhood had a particularly ripe aroma. Somebody was cooking rat soup somewhere nearby, that was certain.

We passed the DeSoto again, and, again, I failed to link myself with it. I wasn't sure why – just my playing at being a private eye, maybe. And I certainly would have told Lana about my ride if she asked. But if not, why not let her think I'd been dropped off in the area by someone? Or taken a cab? Or the bus? What difference did it make?

We got to the door and I was amused as she went through a pantomime of unlocking with her jingling keys the door that had no functioning lock. I understood – I mean, you didn't know who was watching from some dark vantage out there. Might as well let this anonymous potential assailant think the building could be locked up tighter than a drum. But, still, the little performance made me smile. Lana was quite convincing. I decided she surely must have been in show business at some time in her life.

I was about to thank her for the info and say goodnight, when she said, "Come up. I'll make us coffee. We can chat a little more." And when I hesitated slightly, she smiled and added, "I'm still a little nervous, okay? I'd love the company."

Smiling back, I said, "Sure. No problem."

I followed her up to the third floor, trying to avoid staring at the swing of her ex-chorus girl derriere. I really didn't want getting involved with women who were a decade my senior to become some kind of habit.

As we reached the third floor, as we creaked the floorboards on the way to Lana's apartment, we passed Vaughn and Erin's apartment (which I had left unlocked) and I got a sick feeling in my gut. Where was Erin, anyway? Lana had really told me nothing I didn't already know (other than her magician theory). In fact, maybe I knew more than she did. My investigation, so to speak, had hit a dead end. I had no clue how to find out if Erin was alive or dead. And maybe no one ever would. God damn it, anyhow. Poor Erin.

All my pains at not looking at Lana in anything but a neighborly light, notwithstanding, when we got in her place and she turned on the light, she relocked the door, turned a deadbolt, and put on a chain. As if we were in for the night.

The old phrase "'Step into my parlor,' said the spider to the fly" came to mind at once. I could bob and weave, but, my weird life had already taught me, that didn't work for everything.

"Make yourself comfortable, Bobber," said Lana. "Take off your jacket. Have a seat on the couch over there. I can absolutely guarantee there are no rodents living in it. You have to make promises like that living in this neighborhood." We both chuckled. Funny joke. "So, I'll put on the coffee – or. Or would you care for something a little stronger?" She raised her eyebrows meaningfully.

This apartment was somewhat bigger than Three-C across the hall. For one thing, the kitchen had its own little room with a doorway and everything. For another, the bed was not in here in the living room – it too had its own room. Call it a bedroom. I could see the foot of the bed in another, darkened open doorway, the actual door sitting open.

Lana seemed to notice my noticing the bed. She smiled slightly and kept the question in the air with her arched eyebrows.

"Well, what do you have?" I asked evenly. I did not want to yield to her seduction, but it felt like it was happening anyway.

"You like bourbon? I got bourbon."

"Sure, I love bourbon. Yeah, I'll take a finger of bourbon. If you have some. Straight up. I've had enough coffee today, I guess."

"Coming right up," she said. "I've got some decent stuff. I'll join you." She went into the kitchen and I heard the clinking of glassware.

Taking off my jacket, I laid it across a chair set at a small table against the wall. I perched Pa's fedora on top of the jacket.

"Gonna use your washroom while you're getting the booze," I said.

"Mm-hm," she muttered.

I went into the bathroom and got rid of a few cups of coffee. And while washing up, my reflection stared at me again. It seemed to ask, "What the fuck are ya doin'?"

Here is what it suddenly felt like I was doing: I'd come all the way downtown to investigate the disappearance of an old friend. But now, what? I'd gotten a little somewhere with this so-called investigation. And I was getting cold feet. I was jumping at the first distraction, allowing myself to be distracted. Sure this woman was attractive – but did I even want sex now? I'd just had sex this morning with Maeve (a disturbingly similar woman, though Lana did not appear to be married). So, with something so serious on the table, I'm going to use that as an excuse to start gettin' laid with different women morning, noon, and night? So, what's next? You gonna go back to poor Peggy O'Kief with all yer wonderful "findings" and try to use her inevitable gratitude to try to lay her as well? The answer was: of course not! But I hated that I'd even thought of the question.

I dried my hands. I didn't like the way the night was unfolding.

Out in the living room, I should have expected what was there, and yet I hadn't.

The overhead light was off, and the only illumination came from a floor lamp off in the corner. An unseen radio was tuned to something dreamy (I believe the precise recording was Harry James' "Sleepy Lagoon"). The kitchen light was off and the only other source of light was a small glow coming from the now no longer dark bedroom, probably from a bedside lamp.

At the far end of the short couch (call it a loveseat) sat Lana, turned sideways, one leg tucked under the other, facing me. In the hand that rested on her leg she held a glass with a splash of bourbon in it. In the hand that rested on the back of the couch, she held another cigarette, but this one was stuck into a carved ivory holder of modest size, angled up. So, she was not just smoking – she was using the cigarette as a prop, to give her the air of a femme fatale from the movies. She had not changed clothes, but the top couple buttons of her blouse had somehow come unbuttoned exposing an inviting length of cleavage (and nestled cozily in the tip of that cleavage – not visible before – was some kind of colorful stone suspended by a gold chain).

And clearly Lana had refreshed her perfume.

Another splash of bourbon in a glass sat on a low coffee table in front of a vacant spot on the couch. A vacant spot that was intended for me.

"Hi, there," she said huskily. "Come over here. Take a load off, you've earned it."

In the rush of the moment, I moved and sat down, picking up my glass. The little voice I had been talking to myself with in the bathroom mirror now seemed far away and even underwater. Was I crazy? Of course I wanted to get laid.

"*Salud*," she said, holding up her glass.

"*Slàinte*," I said, and we clinked glasses. We drank. It tasted damn good and I held back from just downing the whole thing.

"So," I said, haltingly, "do you have to get up early tomorrow?"

"No," she said fixing me with a dreamy, hypnotic stare. "I work in a bank. But I have tomorrow free. So – what about you? Does the famous Bobber Maxwell have to be anyplace in the morning?"

I had walked right into that one. The idea that my answer of "no" would only get me more entangled in the web of this vamp did not bother me as much as having to admit that I didn't have a job.

Nevertheless, I was about to answer that I had nowhere to be when that image of Peggy crying returned. It was now joined by a mental recreation of the black and white photo featuring Peg and Erin as teenagers.

I decided to bob and weave.

Taking another sip, I said, "Before it gets too late, do you mind if I ask you just a couple more questions about what you were telling me before?"

I could tell she was pissed at my question, but she disguised it expertly. With a pasted on grin, she gripped the cigarette holder in her teeth, sucked in and blew out a stream of smoke from the opposite side of her mouth, and said, "No problem. What do you want to know?"

Plowing ahead, I said quietly, attempting not to wreck the mood Lana had so carefully created, "You said that you thought Erin – and Vaughn too, I guess – might work for a magician. I can't quit thinking of it. I just wonder what about their visitors, or anything, put that idea in your head?"

She carefully set the cigarette and holder in the ashtray on the coffee table and took another sip of her drink. She said, "Well, I don't know exactly. Let me think. I guess it was mostly something I once overheard Erin saying to Vaughn as they came down the hall one day."

"So this was during daylight, during the week? The weekend?"

"I don't remember. I'm pretty sure it was daytime. She said to Vaughn something like 'the applause is never long enough and she never seems like she's gonna get from behind the curtain in time, they need to rehearse that more.' Something like that. Kinda sounded like she was talking about some stage illusion, the kind a magician would do with an assistant, making her disappear or something. You know what I'm saying?" She picked up her cigarette again and took another drag, this time not quite so seductively.

"Yeah," I said. "I do know what you mean. Do you remember what Vaughn answered?"

"No, he mumbled something, but I couldn't understand him. Also, sometimes I would see her come home with very thick make-up on her face, very overdone eyes, rouged cheeks. But when I'd see her just a little while later it would be washed off."

"Okay," I said. "I guess that was really the only other thing I wanted to ask about Erin. Thanks."

"Like I said, not a problem." She had the holder gripped in her teeth again, looking at me expectantly. I guess it was my move.

I downed the rest of my bourbon and carefully set the glass down on the coffee table. No false moves in the den of the lioness.

"Well, thank you so much, Lana. I mean that. For everything. I'm sure we'll see each other soon." There was a longish pause. She had my eyes drilled with hers.

"Would you like another drink, dear?"

"Oh, no. Sounds good, but I've got a long way to drive tonight. All the way back to Canaryville, and all." Another longish pause. I'd never been stared at like this ever before. The hunger in those eyes was palpable.

"You don't have to, you know," she said at last. "Drive."

"I do," I said with all the respect I could muster. I know the field mouse under the talons of the owl is not expected to show the owl respect. I just happen to be a very respectful rodent.

"You can stay here tonight," she said. "I'm inviting you."

"I can't."

"Why?"

"Because I have to drive back. It's important."

"What? Are you married or something? Little woman waiting?" She said this last with a slight sneer.

"No. Nope. Not married. Not one bit. Never have been. Not even going with anyone." It was the truth. I did not count Maeve Hoolihan.

"Then why? I'm inviting you, fer Chrissake."

"Because it's important. You're going to have to trust me when I say that." And then I felt the need to add, "I'm not a liar."

"If you leave right now, I'll hate you."

"I wish you wouldn't. But I still have to go. Goodnight, Lana. Thanks again, and I really mean that."

And on that note, of me really meaning it, I stood, grabbed my hat and jacket, and headed for the door. I undid all the locks and left the apartment, closing the door respectfully and quietly behind me. I had not looked back and, for all I knew, Lana was still sitting in the same position on the couch, angrily chewing on her cigarette holder.

That dark hallway was one spooky place. I moved as though a banshee were nipping at my ass. Out on the street, I felt a little better but not much. The thing for me to do was get to the car.

Walking out onto the middle of Hubbard, I headed right for the DeSoto. This block was pitch black, but I could make out the dark form of the car. When I had been parking in daylight, it did not seem like I had pulled in so far away. I would have welcomed a car just then, beeping at me to get out of the way, its illuminating headlamps showing me the details of the neighborhood. But there were no random vehicles at the moment, and those sidewalks looked dark, dark, dark. The DeSoto still seemed about twenty-five yards away.

Almost on cue, two forms moved from the sidewalk out into the street ahead of me. In my periphery I was aware of a third dark form moving at me directly on my left.

# Chapter Three

I stopped and turned slightly to my left in an attempt to keep all three of these fine upstanding citizens somewhat in front of me.

"Hey, man," said a voice coming from one of the forms ahead of me in the street, "you gonna get hit by a car walking out there. You got any spare change?" The voice had some kind of accent that I couldn't place.

"Naw," I said. "All my spare change goes to the Red Cross."

The guy coming at me from the left was raising his arm. My left hand darted out and up, grabbing his wrist tightly as I buried my right fist in his gut. The air whooshed out of him and I then smashed that right fist into his face. He gave a liquid cry as he gargled his own blood and teeth – and the lead pipe, or whatever, he had intended for my head clanged on the street.

I wished I could have grabbed that pipe because in the next instant the other two guys were upon me.

An unseen switchblade clicked open. I spun, nearly avoiding it, but it caught me in the arm. I landed a wild haymaker right in Switchblade's head and his knife went skittering down the street as he hit a parked car which must have damaged him further.

But that gave the third guy an extra moment or two. As I spun to face him, I felt him launch himself into me with a flying tackle. I grabbed fiercely onto him and pulled him down with me – in case he had any idea of letting go. I landed right on my back and it wasn't pretty, the wind got knocked out of me with Tackler right on top of me. He used this advantage to aim a good one at my face, and he caught me good on my brow, just above my left eye. But I'm used to fighting with the wind knocked out of me – plus, I was plenty mad now. My legs wrapped around him in a vicious scissor hold and he cried out as I surely cracked one of his ribs. Keeping him pinned in place, I found my breath and pummeled his head with both fists till he stopped struggling and went limp. I shoved him onto the pavement.

I dragged myself into a standing position. I could only make out the dark forms of Tackler at my feet and Switchblade on the street next to the car. There was no telling where Lead Pipe had gotten to – maybe he was just lying in a shadow somewhere hidden by the darkness, maybe he had limped off home to pick the fragments of face bone out of his eyes, or maybe he could show up again with his lead pipe, or some other weapon, seething with revenge.

I started to run for the car and realized I felt really banged up. Hopefully I didn't have a concussion. My back hurt like hell. Not only that, but I saw a dark patch on my left jacket sleeve, felt the wetness on my wrist and hand, and realized that jerk had nailed me with that switchblade – perhaps more seriously than I'd realized. I didn't relish the idea of bleeding all over Pa's nearly pristine seat cover. Plus, I didn't feel like driving. I thought of sneaking back into Three-C and cleaning up. But it didn't seem like a great idea to smear my blood around the joint.

All I could think to do was return to Lana's. I saw the outline of my hat on the street, carefully picked it up with my right hand trying not to get blood on it, and plopped it onto my noggin. I shuffled back the way I had come.

It wasn't fun. Those monkeys had messed me up more than I wanted to admit.

Still some distance away from the building, I stopped and fished out my hanky. My arm didn't seem to be bleeding heavily, but I hiked up my jacket sleeve and fashioned a makeshift tourniquet anyway. I didn't want to leave a trail of blood up to Lana's door, either.

The agonizing trudge up to the third floor seemed to take forever. But I made it. And then I was standing in front of Lana's apartment. I knocked softly.

I heard quick footsteps approach the door (it did make me think she'd been sitting in the same position the entire time).

"Who is it?" she asked softly, breathlessly.

"It's just Bobber. I could use a little helping hand."

There was the sound of Lana undoing her system of locks. Then the door was flung wide. She was still dressed the same, but her eyes were puffy and her makeup was smeared. Had she been crying? There was anger in her eyes just then, however, and it looked like she was ready to chew me out – until she saw my blood-soaked sleeve, my swelling eye. She froze in mid-snarl.

"What the fuck, Bobber?" she squealed, showing off a very unladylike vocabulary. "What happened? Never mind that – get in here."

And, using her thumb and forefinger like a pair of tweezers, I thought, she took my jacket by the non-bloody right sleeve, and pulled me into the apartment. She quickly redid the locks.

"I got jumped by three guys out in the street," I said, trying to make the explanation as simple as possible. "Don't worry, they all look a lot worse than I do."

"How badly are you hurt?"

"I think one of 'em got me pretty good with a switchblade there." With a nod of my head, I indicated my left arm.

"Oh lord," she said, leading me into her bathroom which was, again, somewhat bigger than Vaughn's had been, "let me take a look at it. Sit on the toilet seat."

I did, and, in a cooperative effort, we both undid the tourniquet and peeled off my ruined sport coat. Then my ruined shirt and tie. I sat bare-chested and blood-smeared on the toilet. I now held my former bloody tourniquet against the wound to catch any further bleeding. Lana daintily plucked off my hat and stowed it safely on the shelf of her closet.

She returned a moment later and took out a bottle of rubbing alcohol and a box of cotton pads from the medicine cabinet.

"Okay," she said, squatting in front of me like a Major League catcher, "let me look at this."

She gently took the hand that I was using to hold the wound and moved it away. The hanky stayed, glued onto my arm by blood. She uncorked the alcohol, got out a big hunk of cotton, and soaked it. Then she slowly peeled away the hanky and pitched it into a nearby wastebasket.

"Oh, boy," she muttered, and started wiping alcohol around and over the area, trying to get a good look at the actual wound.

I was doing great, but then the alcohol must have seeped in a little deeply and I yelped like a mutt whose tail had been caught under a rocking chair.

"Be quiet!" she snapped, as she continued to stare into the wound. Florence Nightingale she was not.

"Sorry," I said, trying to clam up my brain's reaction to the pain, "I'm usually a lot better behaved after a stabbing."

"Been stabbed a lot, then?" she asked, distracted and mirthless.

"No," I said, not bothering to explain that I'd been trying to make a joke.

"You, baby boy, are going to need some stitches." She said it and left the room. I glanced down at the wound. It was a nasty little slice, a four inch gash on my forearm, that gapped a little too much."

"I'd better be leaving for the hospital then?" I called out.

Without answering, she returned holding an olive drab metal case about a half a foot by a foot in size. There was a white rectangle painted on the lid and a red plus sign painted on top of that.

"I've got a first aid kit," she said matter-of-factly. "I know how to stitch up these things."

I could think of no wisecrack to make as I watched, mouth agape, at the vision of her digging out a pack of needles and a spool of what I could only guess was catgut.

She chose a nasty-looking needle, threaded a modest length of catgut through the eye, then held the sewing assemblage over the sink and doused the whole thing, needle and catgut, in alcohol. Then she looked at me and grinned.

"Hold out your arm. This won't hurt a bit."

"That's a lie, isn't it?"

"Yep. Hold out that arm. Gotta be done."

So, I held out my arm and it got the alcohol too. And, by God, it did hurt. I kept my mouth shut though – I didn't want to give her the satisfaction.

She sewed me up like a prize football. Then she dressed the wound with gauze and adhesive tape. Next she bandaged the area over my eye, and got me some ice in an icebag to hold on it. She gave my back and the back of my head a once over, but said unless I continued to feel pain, I probably wouldn't have to see a doctor. She warned me to keep the knife wound clean.

"Now to put you to bed." I still did not feel like driving (certainly not without a shirt, only to face Ma once I got home), so I let her lead me like a toy balloon into the bedroom.

"Take off your pants and shoes," she ordered, moving to the bedroom closet. The room was neat enough, but not what I would call particularly girly – more practical than anything. There were several stacks of magazines, newspapers, and pulpy looking paperback books here and there, all neatly arranged on the floor or table surfaces. This was the room of a reader.

She pulled out a huge brown terrycloth robe and tossed it at me. "Put that on. It's mine, but it'll fit you, it's gigantic."

I carefully finished taking off my pants and, so I wouldn't be standing there gawking about the room in my boxers and socks, I put on the robe.

"Now, get in the bed. Cover up. I don't want any arguments. Can I get you anything?"

Climbing into bed, I pulled the covers over my legs, but remained in a sitting position. "That cup of coffee doesn't sound half bad right about now. But listen, Lana, you don't, I mean, you've done enough."

"Shut up," she said, "just do what you're told. You've been hurt. I'm helping you. End of story. I'll have some coffee with you."

Have you ever met someone whom your instincts told you you should be afraid of because they might be a little crazy? Well, the loony whistles were definitely going off in my mind right now regarding Lana here. She was helping me, no doubt, and it was help I needed. But she was a very – very – controlling person. And the more time I spent with her, the more questions she raised. Just for example, where did she learn to suture a wound like that, and what was she doing with what looked to be an army first aid kit?

At my very first opportunity, probably when I thought she was asleep, I resolved to sneak out (with my pants and shoes and ruined jacket, but only if possible) and make for my car.

"There's aspirin on the nightstand, and water, if you're feeling some pain," she called from the kitchen as she banged around with the coffee pot.

"Thanks," I called back. "I believe I will take some." There were four or five tablets in the little bedside bottle, and I just emptied it into my mouth washing down the tablets with the room temperature water left in Lana's glass. I wondered idly how long that water had sat there, but there was no point in worrying about that.

She returned a moment later and sat on the edge of the bed. Apparently attempting to improve her bedside manner, she said, "Coffee should be ready soon. So – you wanna tell me what happened exactly?" It was a challenge, as if all I did was try to find ways to hide things from her.

"It's really just what I said when I came in. I'll give you more details if you really want them."

And so I did. This time, I slipped and did mention I'd been heading for my car, but she did not seem to react like my having a car was one of the things I'd been hiding from her – even though it had.

When I finished, she shuddered and said. "Well, I am glad you didn't get yourself killed." That's mighty nice, I thought. "It sounds like you do know how to take care of yourself, though. The creeps will be gone by now. Do you want the cops?"

"Oh, hell, no," I said. "Nothing they could do. Nothing was stolen and I didn't see any faces." I left out about how I didn't want this incident to get all entangled with the reason I came here in the first place, to look for Erin. I got the feeling that even though Lana claimed friendship for Erin, whenever I'd brought her up, Lana seemed to react jealously, as though she were in competition with Erin for – what? For me?

We both smelled the coffee then, and Lana went and got a couple mugs. The java was slightly burnt-tasting, but I wasn't going to start complaining now.

We sat sipping in silence for a while. Then she said, "This neighborhood has gotten so shitty. Stuff like this happens all the time. You see why I wanted you to walk me back from the restaurant? I gotta get out of here."

And I don't blame you, I thought but decided to keep it to myself.

We spoke for awhile longer, finishing our coffee. Then Lana stood and took our empty cups out to the kitchen. And when she came back into the room, she asked me if I needed anything more. I said I was going to visit the bathroom in a bit.

She nodded and said, "Okay, well, I'm running out of steam, somewhat. I'm gonna get ready for bed. It's already close to midnight."

Then she pulled open a dresser drawer and dug out a pair of pink pajamas. To my astonishment, she tossed them on the bed (over my legs to be precise) and undressed right in front of me without apology or ceremony. I was tempted to hide under the covers, but I couldn't look away.

First she undid the rest of her buttons, took off her blouse, and tossed it over a chair. Standing in her bra, she reached behind her back and undid the clasp, letting her semi-huge breasts fall out, the large brown nipples staring back at me like a pair of eyes. She sat on the bed and undid her slacks and pulled them and her panties off a leg at a time. She was not wearing hose of any kind. Allowing everything to show, including her pubic bush, she picked up her pajamas and pulled them on, leaving her pajama top unbuttoned for the moment.

"I'm just gonna pop in the bathroom and quickly brush my teeth before you use the toilet," she said, heading out the bedroom door. "If you want to clean your own teeth, you can just use my brush, I don't care – don't have an extra one. Just rinse it good when you're done."

Things were spiraling out of control. This was one helluva slumber party I found myself in. I sat stunned, listening to her brush her teeth, then gargling and spitting into the sink. I heard the bathroom door shut, and a minute or so later I heard the toilet flush and the door opened again. She came back into the room.

Walking around the foot of the bed, she moved between the side opposite me and the wall that housed a window. She turned on the light of the opposite nightstand and fished a cigarette from a pack lying there. She lit it and got into bed next to me, picking up a nearby magazine and getting all cozy.

"I'm just going to read for a while. Then I'll shut off my light. You can read too, if you want. I've got plenty to read lying all around here."

I quietly got out of bed and hit the bathroom. When I was done, neither did I use her toothbrush nor did I look at my reflection.

Back in the bedroom, Lana was sitting there reading, the cigarette perched between her lips, her left eye squinting slightly from the smoke. She glanced at me and smiled distractedly. She must have been reading something good. The subject of "sleeping arrangements" had never been broached. I decided some broaching was in order.

Hooking my thumb back towards the living room and the loveseat, I said, "Lana, look. I can sleep out on the –"

She set the open magazine down on her lap and spoke with cigarette bobbing in her mouth. "Oh, no, look yourself. You were seriously injured tonight. I'm the one who dressed your wounds, and I know about infections and such. And you are in danger of getting infected if you're not careful. I want to keep a close eye on you all night to make sure you don't develop a fever. Didn't they teach you anything in the army?" She pointed at the spot next to her that I had vacated. She didn't yell, exactly, but she had a manner that left no doubt that she was being serious. "Now don't be a sissy. Get in the Goddamned bed."

"Okay," I grumbled, and got in the bed. I shut off my light and laid on my back carefully, trying to get comfortable, hoping the aspirins would kick in soon. Lana sat there reading, flipping pages periodically. I stared past her, out the window at the moon rising just beyond the fire escape. A flashing sign from somewhere down below provided hypnosis. We were like an old married couple.

Only I was going to be guilty of desertion as soon as I could manage it.

Before too long, Lana stubbed out her cigarette and laid her magazine aside. Shutting off her light, she slid down and got comfortable.

"Goodnight, Bobber," she said quietly.

I grunted an answering response, trying to keep it neutral, resisting the temptation to say, "Good night, Dear."

It is unclear whether it was the flashing hypnotic sign or if Lana had slipped me a Mickey in my coffee (it seemed like perfectly reasonable behavior from what I already knew of her). But I did not stay awake long. Something flipped my switch and I slid deep into some type of slumber – drugged or otherwise.

There was a dream. Some kind of dream you wouldn't be able to recall, even at gunpoint. The one thing I did remember from it is that the dream had turned erotic. And as my mind slowly came back to a kind of dopey wakefulness, I realized that I was being manipulated in some way in the portion of the body where eroticism is born. Someone had their hand inside the terrycloth robe. And it wasn't me.

There was arousal happening despite the throbbing pain in my arm. It was not with my consent, but was happening because of another person. I am no lawyer, but I believe this falls under some definition of rape. I grunted something and started to say her name – and I felt her put her other hand over my mouth. Then she rolled on top of me.

She moved her mouth close to the left side of my head. "After what you did to me before," she whispered throatily into my ear, "I hope you didn't think I was going to sit still for it."

She was completely naked. I felt her remove the hand that was doing the marauding down there and she pulled open the robe with it. Now, many of my naked parts were touching her naked parts.

I won't cry rape, because I lazily let it happen. In the moment it seemed like the easiest thing to do. The path of least resistance. Hardly a virgin I, after all. But it wasn't my idea. I might not be willing to testify to that in court. But it wasn't my idea.

She eventually took her hand from my mouth, but she replaced it smoothly with her own mouth – allowing for no lovers' billing and cooing to take place. I could have easily pushed her off me – with some effort – but I was motivated not to because I feared messing up my newly stitched knife wound. Maybe she was figuring on that. Anyway, to make my final excuse as to why I allowed this to continue – well, she was fucking me, not murdering me (not yet at any rate). God help me, I allowed myself to feel the pleasure rather than struggle.

The violent act completed, she collapsed on top, breathing heavily (we both were). Eventually, she rolled off and back onto her side of the bed, such as it was. Soon she was snoring softly. Though I'd had my share of sexual experiences before, during, and after the war, I had never had one where the woman had been the clear aggressor.

She lay on her stomach, still nude, her big left breast pushing out from under her. I watched her breathing and snoring like this for a while, wondering what the hell had just happened to me (my wound quietly throbbing). Eventually, I must have slid into sleep as well.

It must have been sometime between two-thirty and three in the morning. Some kind of noise woke me. It was still dark in the room but from the dim light filtering in through the window, I could see Lana still next to me. At some point she must have put her pink pajamas back on. She was now on her back, and I was on my left side facing her, my arms still in the robe, and my boxers were still pulled down below my ass from the devilish lovemaking. With a quiet struggle of my right arm, I hiked them back up again. My left arm was sticking out at a weird angle from under me – I must have naturally tried not to roll on my wound during my sleep.

I heard the noise again. It was a quiet, hesitant cracking. My left eye was buried in the pillow, but my right eye, with which I'd been looking at Lana, could see about the room from its limited vantage. And what it now finally saw was the outline of a man out on the fire escape.

He was very still and seemed just to be staring in at us. I guessed from the fact that he had not suddenly flown the coop, that he did not realize my eye was open, had not seen me adjust my shorts. My senses were on high alert now, however, and the longer I stared back at him through the windowpane, the more my eye became accustomed to the dark. And a flash of metal at the bottom of the window told me he had a knife – and he was using this knife to pry the window open.

It didn't make any sense for this to have been one my attackers, come back to finish me off. But if it was my old pal Switchblade – was he ever gonna get a surprise. I could feel the muscles in my body coiling for action as they sucked up the adrenaline I was sending them.

The guy was diligent, I'll give him that. He brought that knife up to the latch at the top of the window, trying to work it open. Then he brought the blade back to the bottom of the window, trying to see if prying the window up would make the latch give. He repeated this sequence a couple times as I watched. I did not want to scare him away. I wanted him to get that window open. In truth, I couldn't wait. I'm like that.

Finally, the guy's persistence paid off. The latch quietly popped open. He paused before going farther, watching to see if he'd awakened us.

I knew I was awake, but if Lana were she was damned good at faking sleep. Sex must have agreed with her.

The period of waiting over, the guy slowly began to raise the window in little increments because it refused to stop squeaking. But eventually, it was all the way up, and a cool breeze wafted across our bodies. This did not wake up Lana either. The guy spied a length of wooden two by two used to prop the window open – which he employed so he no longer had to hang onto the squeaky thing.

Then he climbed nimbly into the bedroom. Inching his way around the bed, he went no further than the foot. Looking at us, he raised the knife above his head.

# Chapter Four

I sprang from the bed, my wound be damned. My head connected with his solar plexus, knocking the wind out of his lungs as if they were a half-inflated balloon let go of before being knotted. My left hand gripped his wrist, shook the knife loose and harmlessly onto the floor. The force of my leap drove us up against the wall. My friend was polite enough to absorb the shock of this with his head, and he collapsed onto the floor with an involuntary groan.

Only then did Lana wake up with a startled cry (not exactly a scream). She turned on her reading light.

Getting out of the bed, she looked at me, blood oozing slightly from under my bandage, standing over an unconscious man lying atop a pile of scattered magazines.

"What the fuck?" she said.

"Exactly," I said, sucking in air. "I better tie up this son-of-a-bitch. How you fixed for rope?"

While Lana got some clothesline from a kitchen drawer, I checked him for I.D. No wallet, no anything. I then tied that sucker good to the chair in the bedroom. We decided to get dressed before he woke up (if he woke up – I'd hit him with everything I had).

Lana threw on a fresh blouse and slacks. She managed to pull a large man's shirt out of her bottom drawer. A memento of a former roommate? I didn't ask. But it fit my big frame. Before I put it on, though, Lana checked my stitches – I had not ripped them, but only caused them to ooze a bit, so that was good.

I was just tying my shoes when the guy groaned. My shoes tied, I walked to the kitchen and got a cup of water. Lana was sitting on the bed smoking a cigarette and watching the guy.

Picking a piece of tobacco off her tongue and flicking it, she said, "What are you going to do? Give him a drink?"

Without ceremony, I grabbed the back of the groaning guy's hair and threw the whole cup of water into his face.

Lana laughed.

"Okay, asshole," I said, "what's the big idea? Talk!"

He was in his twenties, in a black windbreaker zipped up halfway over a white tee shirt. He wore chinos and sneakers. He appeared to be white but with some kind of Asian blood mixed in there.

He spat and coughed water. When that subsided and he appeared to be conscious again, I repeated my questions. He did not speak, but shifted his eyes between Lana and me with great fear.

"Do you recognize this piece of shit?" I finally asked Lana.

She dragged on her cigarette thinking about it. She stared at the intruder carefully – even warily. He returned her gaze with genuine terror.

At last she said, "I think I've seen him. Maybe in the neighborhood. Sure, you know he might be one of those characters I saw visiting Vaughn and Erin recently."

"Yeah, asshole?" I said, thinking of the photograph again, letting the image fuel my anger. "You know Erin O'Kief?"

He continued to look terror-stricken, glancing rapidly between Lana and myself. When he had stood at the foot of the bed, he had looked like he was about to stab Lana. Now he looked like he himself was about to be killed.

"I'll tell ya," said Lana. "I'm not sure he even speaks English."

I took a good look at him. He was trembling, but I got the idea he understood at least part of what we were saying.

"I don't know about that." And then I decided to test something. I picked up the knife off the floor. It was not a switchblade but a small hunting-type knife with a five inch blade. "Maybe we should just kill him, instead."

Our friend definitely flinched as I said that. Lana chuckled. "Well, he sure understood that."

"No, we won't kill you. But, really, the only thing to be done is to call the police and have them haul you away."

Lana's brow furrowed as I said this.

"I don't really want to either, but what choice do we have? I mean, if we aren't gonna kill him, what else are we going to do? Breaking and entering? Attempted murder?"

"All right," the guy suddenly said, "I'll talk. I'll talk. Just please don't call the cops."

After an astonished pause, I said, "Well, okay. I'm not promising anything. But what do you have to say?"

"Untie me first. Please. I'm scared to death yer gonna kill me. Please. I'll talk, I promise. I just want to feel in control"

"We can't untie him," said Lana, flatly. "The fuckhead pulled a knife on us."

The guy was trembling, looking at Lana as if she were already cutting his throat. She had that lioness' glare staring at him, and I almost pitied the idiot.

"No one's getting untied just yet," I chuckled, amazed at his nerve. "What's your name, asshole? Let's start with that."

Again he was looking back and forth between us. "Cappy," he finally said. "I'm Cappy."

"Okay, now we're getting somewhere," I said. "Cappy, you say?" He nodded his head, but didn't speak again. "Like I already asked you, Cappy, do you know someone named Erin O'Kief?"

Again, he just stared, with that dumb terrified look. I suddenly had an inspiration. The last time I'd laid eyes on Erin, she still looked a lot like she had in high school – a lot like that photo I'd found. Maybe it was just her name that Cappy didn't recognize.

"Where did you stash my sport coat?" I asked Lana.

"I rinsed the blood off the sleeve and hung it up in the living room closet. It's still torn."

Exiting the bedroom, I opened the closet. The coat was indeed hanging there, ripped sleeve and all – and the sleeve was still a bit damp. I pulled it on anyway, and, seeing my hat on the shelf, I put that on too. I still was hoping I could exit this place soon if at all possible. And I sure didn't want to start talking to the police now. With Cappy in tow, however, I wasn't sure if that would be possible.

As I reentered the bedroom, Lana was still having a staring contest with Cappy. She was winning.

"Here," I said, reaching down into my inner pocket and pulling out the photo (I was glad it was still there). Maybe this will help shake up your memory.

I'd only just started to show our captive the photo, when movement at the window drew my attention. I looked up and saw another man, dark-haired but not particularly Asian-looking, standing there on the fire escape. We locked eyes for a moment and this time Lana did indeed scream.

In that instant, the guy bolted and we heard the rapid-fire sound of his feet on the metal steps.

"Secure this window and keep an eye on this guy!" I yelled. "Hopefully, I'll be back!" And, shoving the photo back in my pocket, I vaulted out the window. I could just make out Lana voicing some kind of protest. But it was too late. Her voice faded, and there were now two sets of footsteps rattling loudly down the fire escape steps.

The guy got about halfway down the final flight and then leaped to the sidewalk. I followed suit, but by the time I was on the pavement, he already was nearly half a block ahead, travelling east on Hubbard. I made chase.

He was nearing Rush Street which was fairly illuminated, comparatively. But before he got there, I could just make out that he had dodged to the right into an alley. I covered the distance quickly, but when I reached the same alley, I entered it but hug the buildings to the right side. There were dim lights at irregular intervals so I tried to keep against the walls and stay in shadow as much as possible. But I would see the silhouette of my quarry up ahead, running at full tilt. I hoped that if he glanced back, he might think he had eluded me. But I kept pace.

I knew we had to be getting close to the river. Sure enough, as he emerged out of the alley and onto a small lane that led to Rush again, I could see the Chicago River lights and the reflection of water on the far wall. I exited the alley just in time to see him reach Rush then turn to the right on a path that seemed to lead to the river.

As I reached the place where he had turned, I just caught sight of his head disappearing down a flight of steps that hugged the left side of a gray building that, in turn, hugged the water's edge. It was the first of a collection of similar three and four-storied buildings that lined the river off to the right. Big square monsters, built earlier in the century right on the river, no doubt, so the waste of whatever the owners of these buildings were up to could be dumped directly into the water and forgotten about.

I'd been able to see my quarry descending those steps by the light of a single streetlamp that stood guard solemnly at the start of this bleak house row.

If I were going to descend those steps also, there would be no avoiding that streetlamp. And I was determined to follow the little dirtbag. I had the feeling that Cappy did indeed know Erin. And if this guy was Cappy's partner, more than likely, he knew Erin as well. There was even a chance Erin may be in that very building and in a lot of trouble.

No, even though I had rarely felt so exhausted, I was going down those steps.

There were several windows along that side, but they were all dark, and I trusted to luck that anyone on the other side of the glass would be sound asleep. Strolling boldly into the light, I reached the top of those steps. The stairway was concrete and the light didn't last long. Abutting the back of this building was a river wall, and you could see the surface of the river on the other side, smelling of dead fish and mystery horrors. Those stairs descended into a concrete stairwell, and whatever cellar or first floor to which those stairs led was level with or even below the river's surface. There certainly were rats in attendance too. You could count on that.

No longer running, Cappy's pal essentially cornered, I started down the steps at a slow pace, keeping my footfalls as quiet as possible.

Once I dropped below the level of the streetlamp light, I could just make out that the stairs led down to a concrete landing and a very black-looking door.

When I reached the landing, I took a deep breath of river air and laid a hand on the door. I gave a hesitant shove with my fingers and the door swung open, unlocked. It did so soundlessly with nary a squeak. There was no light at all in there and the inky maw beckoned me enter. There was an acrid smell wafting out of the place that stung the eyes. Opium? Some sort of seafood dish? I did not recognize it, though there was a vague familiarity about it.

My fingers reached into my pants pocket and I found my lighter. I was just about to pull it out and give myself some brief illumination when there came a blow behind my right ear, and the blackness from beyond the door flooded my mind as well.

# Chapter Five

What? What is that, I thought. What the hell am I feeling?

I began to suck in a deep breath of air and found out I couldn't because I was underwater.

Something was pulling me down. I tried to kick my legs and discovered that they had been bound somehow at the ankles. I tried reaching down only to further learn that my wrists were tied as well. Testing and pulling at my wrists, the piece of rope (?) came apart and floated away. This clearly had been a hasty job. Lucky for me. I only hoped the ankles were as hasty.

I reached down for my ankles and all at once I felt my downward motion halt and was aware of a thunking kind of noise in my ears – as though whatever invisible weight that was pulling me down had reached the bottom. I explored with my fingers and found that a belt was wrapped around my ankles and the weight was attached to this belt by a rope – a rope now pulled taut.

I struggled with the belt for one panicky moment, but it too let go of me when I discovered the buckle and undid it.

Immediately, I slowly rose towards the surface. Kicking, I sped the process along, my lungs about to burst. Creepy things floated past and brushed against me in the dark, and I tried not to think of what they were. I kept kicking and stroking with my arms to reach blessed, delicious air.

Just when I thought I had no ability left to hold my breath, I broke the surface. Extremely aware that the person or persons who had tried to drown me may still be nearby watching, I attempted to make my coming to the surface as silent an event as possible. The lungful of wonderful smelly river air was sucked in with the greatest restraint also.

It took a moment to get my bearings; I was slowly being swept by the current in the direction of Lake Michigan. Not wanting to go there, I grabbed a pylon of an approaching pier and hung on. The back of my head throbbed where I'd been slugged.

From the direction which I had floated, I heard voices. Two men were standing on the next pier over staring down at the water in front of them. In the limited light, it did not appear that they had noticed me surface. I moved carefully behind the pylon and watched them. One was average-size but the other was some kind of giant. I was certain that these were the parties responsible for the watery attempt on my life. They must have been waiting to make sure I was really gone. Well, ha ha, fellas.

I could only make out snatches of words they were saying. "Shipment." "Client." "Makes it difficult." I had no context in which to insert these words. But there was a name I heard repeated by each of the men a couple times.

"Madame Hilda."

I heard no mention of Erin's name. This could end up being a wild goose chase. But I didn't think so.

Eventually, they must have decided that my goose was cooked, and they climbed a ladder to the top of the river wall. I lost sight of them but heard a door shut. They must have gone inside and I was very happy about it as my teeth had begun to chatter uncontrollably. I wanted out of the cold water.

I wasn't about to return to the dock from which I'd been pitched, so I inspected the one I was under. Along the river wall, on the far side, a thin wooden stairway led down to a loose platform that floated, attached to the stairway by a chain, so the platform could change levels freely with the level of the river on any given day. I swam to this platform and pulled myself onto it. The moment I was out of the water, I rolled onto my back. A wave of nausea rolled over me. The next instant I was leaning back over the water and vomiting. All that lovely restaurant food, Lana's bourbon – and for what? But the purge made me feel instantly better.

So, slowly getting on all fours, I dared to move into a crouch and then a standing position. The bottom of those steps hovered about three feet above my floating platform. Gripping the iron handrail sunk into the concrete wall, I pulled myself up and onto the stairs.

Soaking wet, I trudged up those steps and onto the top of the dock – then I scaled the attending ladder up the wall and onto the top of it. There was no house at the top of this wall, only a muddy path. With only a brief glance at the house I had tried to enter, I got out of there.

Rather than seek out that alley, I decided to pick up Hubbard again by taking Rush Street where there were at least some Goddamned streetlights. I had no idea what time it was, but it was still dark out. So far, it had been a hell of a night.

Along the way, I took stock of my belongings. My car keys, house keys, and change all seemed to be in my pockets. Same with my pen knife and lighter. I didn't want to mess with the picture of Erin (and that magazine page showing the snake) till I could figure out how to dry them properly, but they seemed to be there as well. Clearly, my buddies had pitched me into the river as if it were more important for me to go away than to even find out who I was.

The only casualty of the experience was my hat – Pa's old fedora. It was either in the drink or my assailants had it. One of them might even be wearing it right now – posing in the mirror, checking out his new chapeau. There was a tug of regret there. But I was overdue to buy a new hat anyway; my one and only fedora I'd had as an adult, the one I'd worn to boot camp, had vanished just there somewhere in the bowels of Camp McCoy.

I turned onto Hubbard, getting closer to Lana's and the DeSoto. I was tempted to just drive away. Trouble was, I'd left her guarding Cappy. That was a genuine problem. Why exactly did I resist the idea of the police?  Certainly their help in locating Erin would be extremely useful despite what they might think of Colin O'Kief.  Then the realization hit that I was afraid – because of my former boxing reputation – that they would recognize me.  And if they did, they would at once make all the wrong assumptions as to what I was doing in Lana's bed with her – if we all told the absolute truth about how we came to meet our friend Cappy.  And, God help me, the image of myself, the hero of Canaryville, was precious to me.  Most of the time, as of late, it seemed to be all I had.

Fuck it, I thought.  The only thing that can be done is to take my lumps.

Reaching Lana's building, I entered and dragged my soaky self up the three flights.  As I shuffled down the hall, teeth still chattering, Lana must have heard me coming because she flung the door of her apartment open and stared at me wild eyed.

"You've been gone for nearly two hours.  It's almost dawn.  Where have you been."

"Our friend invited me for a swim," I said.  "I've been pearl diving."

Finally focusing on my condition, she said (all Florence Nightingale again), "Oh! You're soaking wet! Your teeth are chattering, you're gonna catch pneumonia. Get in here, we need to get you out of those things and back into bed. Oh, my God, your stitches!"

"My stitches will be fine. First things first – how's Cappy? You got him napping in there?"

"No," she said, looking stricken, "he's gone. He got away from me."

Neat trick, Cappy, I thought. Care to share some tips? But what I said out loud was, "What the fuck, Lana?"

"Don't shout at me," she said, rubbing the back of her own head. "He hit me."

She indicated for me to step into the apartment – which I did – but, even though she sat on the loveseat, I remained standing. I didn't want to listen to her explanation out in the hall where anybody might overhear it – but I also wanted to be ready to bolt.

Evidently, after I'd left, about fifteen minutes went by in awkward silence. Then Cappy asked to be allowed to go to the bathroom. Not wanting him to just mess himself there in her bedroom, she agreed to cut only the ropes that secured him to the chair and lead him like a dog to relieve himself. On the way, however – according to Lana – he freed his hands and hit her (this surprised me since I thought I had knotted him up good at the wrists).

Cappy nailed her in the back of the head, shoving her onto the floor. Then he ran from the bedroom and out the front door. She saw him from the bedroom window running down the street in the same direction I had gone.

"I didn't know what else to do, so I just sat here holding ice on my head, waiting for you. He didn't take his knife though. I still have it, see?" Attempting pride in herself, she indicated the knife on the coffee table.

"Good. Keep it." I said. "You might need it sometime." I looked for an ice bag but saw none. Her hair did not appear wet from melted ice, but I couldn't see the back of her head either.

"I know I messed up," she said. "I'm just not used to being in a situation like that."

"It's okay, you did good. There's really no reason to call the police – unless you really want to report your assault?" She shook her head no and chuckled.

"I know he broke in and wanted to kill me. But we'd have to get into the whole tying him up part… cops aren't going to do anything in this neighborhood."

"All I ask is if you could leave my name out of it if possible. Or whatever you decide. I have to go." I didn't completely agree about the helpfulness of the police, but I also didn't want my name given to them.

"Oh, Bobber, won't you please get out of those wet clothes, let me take a look at your stitches."

"Like I told you before, I really have to go – especially now, before things get fucked up royally. I'll be in touch soon to compare notes. If there are any notes to compare. Good night, or, I suppose, good morning."

I turned, knowing full well she was sitting there doing a slow burn. I didn't care. The living room closet was sitting open and I saw my tie dangling there on the hanger that my coat had been on. It was the sole item of my clothing that had avoided the river dunking. I grabbed it as I made my swift exit. I knew Lana must be plenty angry at my refusing to play doctor with her again. But there was no way I was getting back in that bed. I doubted she would call the police. She didn't seem any more anxious to see them than I did.

As I reached the DeSoto, I dug out its keys, and I was mighty glad to have them. I half expected the car to be up on blocks and the wheels gone. But everything seemed unmolested this time. It was more than I could say for myself.

There was a folded up chamois on the floor of the backseat that Pa had used to polish his new car. It still smelled like Simoniz. I unfolded it and spread it over the front seat where my ass would perch in an attempt to keep the river water off it. I took off my ripped and puckered sport coat and laid that on the floor of the backseat in the chamois' place.

As I played with the clutch, as the DeSoto moaned to life, I realized the sky looked lighter in the East, and the outline of things around me looked more defined, more "visible."

I cast a glance up Hubbard to Lana's building. With my eyes, I followed the fire escape up to the third floor and to what must be her bedroom window. I could just make out a dark form there and the tiny red glow of a cigarette.

Moving forward, I drove quickly past her building, taking a left onto Rush, and a quick right onto Illinois Street. The first right turn off Illinois had me onto Michigan Avenue again, and the

Tribune Tower sped past me on the left this time. Over the bridge and south I went.

South to Canaryville and some fun times trying to explain where I'd been to Ma. Honestly, I may have been more scared of her than anyone I'd ever faced in the ring.

# Chapter Six

I didn't make a huge amount of noise, but there was no point being overly quiet. Stealth would get me nowhere, only luck could save me. But why should I start getting lucky now?

I got the old DeSoto stored away safely in the garage. It had done a good job for me and I was grateful the bottom of it hadn't fallen out somewhere along the line. I would have Jerry give it a more thorough once over very soon.

The sun was already low in the eastern sky by the time I was walking up our back flagstone walk, but the neighborhood had not fully awakened yet. The birds were louder than any people at this point. All the wash had been taken in and the gray clothesline swung empty in the morning breeze like so many jump ropes.

I unlocked the backdoor and shut it behind me as naturally as I could. It was one thing to act like I was just being considerate – but you just didn't want to appear to be "sneaking in" in front of Ma. She would shoot first and ask questions later, as they say.

On my way through the living room, I saw her lying on the couch, deep in slumber. I walked with confidence to the stairway. But I hadn't even made my first double step up when a voice stopped me.

"Now what the hell happened ta ya? Ya look like ya bin ridin' a glashtin. Jayzus Keerist."

I turned, and in the pause she was allowing me, I said, "I been out all night lookin' for Erin, Ma." That stopped her.

"Oh, bloody hell, Roderick," she said at last. "Ya didn't find her, did ya?"

"No, but I think I have an idea where she might be – if she's not – you know." I started to sit in Pa's chair, but thought better of it. Ma grabbed the sheet she had been sleeping under and tossed it over the chair.

"Here, sit on dis. I'll just pitch it in the next load o' wash."

I sat on the sheet, and Ma sat back on the couch.

"So, what happened to yer? Why do ya look and smell like that?"

"Well, I been hit with a lead pipe, punched in the eye, stabbed in the arm, and tossed in the river to drown. Just yer average good time in the city."
I left out the part about being raped by an

Amazon. There's only so much a guy can share with his mother.

"Stabbed?" she asked, getting to her feet. I showed her the sodden bandage under the shirt Lana had given me (I did not explain where this strange shirt had come from, and she didn't ask – but being the main handler of my laundry, surely she noticed), and she peeled it off me inspecting the soggy stitches. I filled her in with a sketchy and short version of the night's events since I had left the house.

As I talked, she fussed over the stitches and I explained (fibbed) that a woman in Erin's apartment building, who had once been an army nurse, did the honors. Ma led me to the sink, produced a large and ancient brown bottle of iodine, and poured a generous amount over the stitches. I'm sure it did me some good, but it stung so bad I yelped, tears forming in my eyes. Whee, Jesus. It for sure hurt worse than the switchblade that had caused the wound.

I blew on the iodine (which had already turned my skin a weird orange) to help dry it. Then I sat back down on Pa's chair and continued my abbreviated tale.

When I finished, Ma whistled a distressed little tweet. Then she said, "So the boyfriend was murdered, huh?"

"Yeah. And the cops don't seem to know his girlfriend was Erin. The thing is, if she is still alive, she isn't safe. If she's in the hands of the people who killed Vaughn Picout, then she's in some pretty ruthless hands. Doesn't seem like they'd hesitate to just toss her in the river – like they did me – just to get her out of the way. So I'm very hesitant to go to the police – yet, anyway. What if some uniformed Mick comes bangin' on their door just on the strength of what I said – they see him through the window and they ditch poor Erin. I mean, it's a real consideration."

Ma was rolling this idea around in her mind, but I was happy that she seemed to agree with me.

"Yeah, Roderick, yer right. I mean, there's some lovely Irish boys on the force okay – but dem coppers got their own way o' tinkin'. Same goes wit tellin' the O'Kiefs. Ya get that Colin – bless his big dumb heart – stormin' over there wit his brudder Peewee. Hell, half the O'Kiefs could be dead by the end of the day."

That's exactly what I was thinking. I had played detective, and I had found out valuable information in the hope of getting Erin home safely. But, in doing so, I had made myself the lone paladin. I was the only one who could use this information safely – and even I had nearly been killed in the process.

"Same with Mr. O'Kief," I agreed. "You know he would want to go over there and bust some heads, and who could stop him? We can't let him risk his life either."

"It's a problem, Roderick. I'm stuck."

"Well, I've got to go up and sleep for a couple hours, then shower and grab something to eat. But I'm probably going back into town again later today. I wish Erin would just show up at her parents' house on her own."

"Amen," said Ma. And in the time it took me to ease my stiff body out of Pa's chair, grab my puckered sport coat, and head for the stairs, Ma handed me a plate of cookies.

She patted my arm. "Yer a good boy, Roderick. I'm sorry we had words yesterday."

I didn't really want to get into it, but I figured I owed it to her. "That thing with Maeve, Ma? Don't concern yourself any more."

Without missing a beat, she smiled and said, "This nice nurse girl who stitched yer arm. She single?"

I just chuckled and shook my head. Sticking a cookie in my mouth – oatmeal – I headed upstairs. A meeting between Ma and Lana was not something I'd care to see.

Upstairs, I barely had the energy to set the cookies on my nightstand, pull the shade against the morning sun, shut the door, and pull off my clothes. I somehow got into fresh boxers, but I seemed to be asleep before I even finished falling into bed. I never even heard the bedsprings squeak.

There was a dream. It was a serious kind of dream. All I ever could remember of it was that I had something to do but couldn't do it. It was one of those frustration dreams. What I remember clear as a bell was that it ended with a tap-tap-tap on my bedroom door.

Ma's voice was saying, in the quietest tone I'd ever heard her use, "You awake, boyo? Roderick?"

"Yeah, Ma," I said into my saliva-soaked pillow. "I'm awake."

The door opened a crack. "I just thought you'd like to know it's a little after noon. You bin sawin' lumber for around six hours now. Is dat enough fer ya?"

I looked up and saw her head poking into the room. On the occasions that usually drove her up here she always seemed to want to box my ears or thrash me in some other way. I smiled at her uncharacteristic angelic expression.

"Yah, Ma, it's enough."

"Whyncha shower and dress. I'll make yer some eggs."

"That sounds good, Ma. Be right down."

I used to have to shower in the basement, or bathe in the claw-footed tub in the bathroom off the kitchen. I still thought of that bathroom as a new thing, even though Pa had put it in where a pantry had been only a couple years after moving in here.

But a couple years before the war, when my prizefighting career was on track, Pete had put a mini-bathroom in the corner up here for me, complete with tiny sink, tiny toilet and very skinny shower stall. I could barely fit in it, but the benefit was I no longer had to shower in the basement. Good old Pete Hoolihan. He'd done it for free. What the hell had I been thinking?

I had to be careful with my stitches, but soon I was cleaned up good and proper, smoothly shaved, and ready for a late breakfast. I was choosing not to think about what lay ahead the rest of the day.

Before going downstairs, I pulled the contents of my coat pocket out and set the items on my little desk next to the window. I raised the shade and let them bathe in the sunlight that flooded the room.

The would-be drowners had left me my wallet. It was just moist on the outside, and my cash, license, etcetera, were only damp around the edges. I spread it all out and let everything bask in the rays.

Birdie the Waitress' napkin was pretty much destroyed. A lump of papier-mâché. I didn't need it anymore, so I pitched it into the waste basket. The photo and glossy magazine page were a little wrinkled but had survived well (though the remains of the toilet paper I had wrapped the page in now hung in a few white strands of nothingness). Setting the photo of the O'Kief family aside for the moment (I really couldn't take looking at it yet), I carefully unfolded the picture of the snake. There was that word, Fer-de-lance.

I got the appropriate volume from my encyclopedia set (a collection of books I had not laid hands on since high school) and looked it up.

All I learned from my crappy little encyclopedia was that this was indeed the name of the snake in the picture. These snakes came from Central and South America. And they were highly poisonous. Very extremely highly poisonous.

This seemed significant, but I could not figure how. This gathering of clues was ridiculously hard. I filed the information away in my noggin and went downstairs.

Ma was waiting in the kitchen for me. There was nothing cooking, but she did have the skillet out and a bowl of eggs sat on the counter.

"I'll get ya some food in a sec, Roderick. But come down in da basement – I need ta go through some tings wit yer." Now this was a more familiar version of Ma. She was in her "evasive" mood. When she was in this mood, one could expect to be ambushed by a smack in the back of the head. But no such ambush occurred.

I followed her down the interior cellar steps. The limestone walls were dank and slightly mossy. I noted that a couple of the old brown stairs could use replacing, and I made a mental note to see to replacing them.

I had to duck not to smack my head on the low ceiling beams. I'd had to duck my head down here since Eighth Grade. Ma pulled the chain that turned on the light bulb which hung over Pa's old workbench.

To my surprise, Ma had Pa's old revolvers laid out on display. All his handguns. I knew how to shoot them, but I'd always hated them – even before joining the army.

"I used yer father's kit to clean 'em up fer yer," she said with the pride of a mother who keeps a clean house. Pa loved his guns, it was a kind of collection. Mainly, he liked to hunt and taught me how, but I'd never had much stomach for it. Besides his shotguns and rifles, he'd also made a point of teaching me to shoot at beer bottles and tin cans with these pistols.

There was his beloved Colt, his Smith & Wesson, a Walther, and, his least favorite, his Webley. Ma had them lined up like cold dishes at a church picnic.

"What is this, Ma? Why are you showing me Pa's guns. I liked them better knowing they were locked away."

142

"I know how to shoot these, ya know," Ma said with pride. "Yer father made sure of it."

"But why show them to me now?"

Ma looked at me very seriously. She put a hand on my forearm. "Roderick, look. I got ta tinkin' while yer were sleepin'. If yer gonna be sneakin' around wit dangerous characters, people whats got no problem wit pitchin' yer in da drink or beatin' yer wit a pipe, well – son, ya need ta have some pertection. I know ya kin lick anyone wit dem fists a yers, but, son, dem types don't fight fair. You tink dem coppers go down ta those places wit nothin' but a smile and a how'd ya do? No, they're packin' heat – and so better you be if yer really gonna help poor Erin."

Of course my first impulse was to disagree with her. But as I stood there staring at the buffet of pistols she had prepared for lunch, I couldn't help feel that her argument made a lot of sense.

"You're right, Ma. I could've used one of these last night. Is there – "

There's boxes o' bullets for each one in da cabinet."

My hand went right for the Colt. It was a .38 and had been the one I'd liked best (or maybe hated least). It was Pa's favorite after all.

143

I spun the barrel out and held it to the light. "Looks like you did a good job cleaning this, Ma. I guess I'll take the Colt here."

"I'll getcha a box o' ammo. Oh, and da Colt fits Pa's shoulder holster."

She got the box of .38 caliber bullets and the holster. "Now, I'll make yer dem eggs," she said and carried ammo and holster up the steps. I followed with the Colt itself.

Ma made great scrambled eggs. I got the works, in fact: bacon, homemade rolls, orange juice. And a couple pots of coffee. When I was done, I felt like I was alive again.

Ma put a fresh bandage over the wound. She declared it healing well with no evidence of any creepy-crawlies from the river having gotten in there. She also declared my eye and brow as needing nothing more than time for the swelling to go down. She also made another reference to the nice nurse I had met, but I ignored it.

A fresh change of clothes (I had switched to my Sunday suit and a new tie) and I was ready to hit the streets. The fedora was lost and Pa's other ones were too beat up and old looking, so I put on my herringbone cap so my head wouldn't feel naked.

I had the shoulder holster on under my jacket (Ma had told me when Pa was a foreman he would wear a pistol to the steel mill just in case trouble should break out), and the Colt was sitting under my arm, loaded and feeling alien. The safety was on and I hoped it still worked.

Out in the garage, I stuck the box of bullets under the DeSoto's front seat, and I had the garage doors flung wide and was about to bring the car out, when I had a visitor.

She very deftly popped around the left side door and came up to the driver's side.

"Going out for a drive?" she asked.

"That's right, Maeve," I said. "What can I do for you?"

The words seemed stuck in her throat, then Maeve blurted out, "You're going out searching for Erin still?"

I was totally flabbergasted. "Yeah, I am. How did you know?"

She tugged at a button on her yellow sweater. "Well, her going missing was all over the neighborhood yesterday. I mean, with her parents going door to door, poor things. And then I ran into Peg at Slattery's." Ah, I thought, so that was it.

"What did Peggy have to say about the situation?" I asked, slightly vexed that Maeve, of all people, was giving any nosy neighbor something else to jabber about her and myself. If Ma's friend Mabel had seen Maeve coming down the alley, she was probably on the phone with Ma right now.

"In a nutshell, she mentioned how you were going to look around. Check your connections in the city." Even though I was trying to keep the brim of my cap pulled down, I saw Maeve wince at my bruised eyelid. "Find out anything?"

"Some things. But not much. Our Erin is in real trouble, I'm afraid. I'm just tryin' to find out where she had been working when —"

"Hey," said Maeve, "I might know something about that. Just popped into my mind, I'd kinda forgotten about it. Erin came over to our place to get Pete not that long ago, a couple months maybe. They had some kind of break in their water pipes and were desperate. While Pete went down in the cellar to get some tools, I was just chewing the fat with her. She happened to mention that she had discovered this wonderful fortune teller woman that she had been going to. Said the woman had wanted her to come work for her."

"What was the name of this fortune teller?" I asked, suddenly interested.

"Well, that's the thing. I don't think I'll ever forget. She told me 'Madame Hilda.' And a chill went down my spine. I'd been to see a Madame Hilda in a little storefront place about a year ago. Me and a friend of mine, Sally Townes, had been shopping and were just wandering around the Tribune area, looking for maybe someplace to eat. We saw this fortune teller place and I thought we should go in and have our palms read, just for fun. Sally saw a shoe store she wanted to go in, so I went to Madame Hilda's by myself. Let me tell you, it was strange from the word go. She was this tall old broad, gray hair, turban, big hoop earrings. Storybook. Before she read my palm, had me sit down, wanted to know everything about me. She had this creepy guy get us cups of tea. As we talked she stared at me so strangely with her weird eyes. I chatted with her, going along with the gag, ya know. I was sipping the tea, and then," Maeve shuddered.

"What? What happened?"

"It was the tea, I think," she continued. "I started feeling strange. Kinda sleepy – weird. I hadn't even had half the cup, but I looked down at it in my hands and a light dawned. I thought, hey, I think I'm being drugged. And the thought scared the shit out of me."

"What'd you do?"

"I got out, that's what I did. I just stood up, feeling a bit woozy, excused myself, and turned my back on Old Staring Eyes. I got out on the street and made a beeline for the shoe store. Sally was trying on some pumps, and she asked me how it was. I was so shook up, I didn't want to talk about it. I just said I never went through with it, chickened out. So Erin says this wonderful fortune teller is called Madame Hilda. I could've shit. I said, oh no, Erin, you can't see her. She's trouble. I just stammered. I couldn't form words. But I could tell I'd said the wrong thing, ya know? Erin started acting a little offended. And then Pete came up with his tools. And they left for her house."

"So, you never told her all you just told me?"

"No, I couldn't spit it out. You're the first person I've ever told."

"Where was this place, Maeve?"

"Oh, God, I don't remember exactly. Just on Rush Street, I'm pretty sure. One of the blocks near the Tribune, you know, near the river there."

Oh, I knew.

"Thank you, Maeve, this might turn out to be important. I gotta go."

I felt like hell just leaving. For one thing, I needed to make sure she knew that she and I were through. Looking at the tears forming in her eyes, I kind of got the feeling she already knew the score.

"Do me a favor, Maeve, shove those garage doors shut when I go. Talk to you soon."

And without looking back, I drove the DeSoto out of the alley and onto the street.

The first stop was the bank. After renewing my membership at Cully's Gym, I was nearly out of money and I had to be able to feed myself. I had no way of knowing what was ahead, and I had to keep up my strength. I went inside and took out a little bit from my savings. There wasn't much left in that account either.

Then I drove over to Tim's hoping I would find Peggy. But as I walked up to the building I caught a glimpse of my reflection in the front window. I didn't like what I saw. In my suit and tie, with my broad shoulders and my cap pulled down over my brow, I just looked like any dumb Mick bully, maybe in the employ of a bookie like Micky, on his way to beat up some poor guy who welched on a bet. I pulled the cap off. No one cared if you went bare-headed into Tim's, anyway. I tossed the cap like a discus into the open window of the DeSoto.

I went inside.

There was a smattering of greetings, but the Sox were playing on the radio again and most attention was being paid to them. Over by the phone booth, however, I saw Peggy. Maxine was in the booth, making a call, and Peggy was leaning on the outside waiting for her.

I caught her eye – and I have to say, her face lit up. I only wished I had something better to tell her. As I walked over, her expression fell when she got a better look at my kisser.

"Bobber, yer eye!" she said, reaching out to pet at it without touching it.

"It's nothing," I said. "Don't even hurt. Listen, Peg. I think I've learned something about where Erin might be. Might be. Please remember I said it that way, because there's nothing certain about anything I've learned."

"I understand," Peggy said, quickly pulling a cigarette out of her purse. I produced my lighter (even though I didn't smoke anymore, I still carried it around with me everywhere I went) and held it out for her. She leaned into the proffered flame and drew in smoke. Exhaling it in a sharp burst, she said (steeling herself for more bad news) "No, I understand. So what's been going on? How did you get hurt?"

I very briefly told her a highly edited version of events, similar to the one I'd told Ma. We had walked some distance from the booth to be out of anyone's earshot, but even though Maxine was still on the phone, I could see her in there eying us curiously.

With the telling of the tale, Peggy's eyes would widen at certain parts as if she were listening to an episode of Inner Sanctum – but she waited to speak. I ended with the piece of information I'd just learned from Maeve. There was just the faintest trace of reaction in her eyes when I mentioned Maeve by name, and I could just tell she'd heard the gossip too. So be it, I would just have to take my lumps – even if the scuttlebutt reached Pete eventually.

When I'd finished my bit, Peggy said, "Aw, Bobber. Christ Almighty. They tried to drown yer? Oh, Honey, you can't be goin' up against those lunatics by yourself. Think of yer Ma. I don't want to tell Henrietta that her boy got killed helping the O'Kiefs!" She laid her hand on my left forearm, right on the wound. I gently moved out of her grip – I had not included the switchblade part into her version of the narrative.

I grabbed her forearms instead. I said with as much intensity as I could quietly muster, "It's okay. Ma knows what I'm doing. She's in favor of it. But I wanted to ask you to please, please, please don't tell anyone what I've told you – not just yet, anyhow. The way I figure it, if that weird place is seen to be under siege, and Erin is still alive in there, well her life won't be worth a plug nickel. They know how to get rid of people in the blink of an eye. If Colin or Peewee – or your dad go –"

"Oh Colin," she said, rolling her eyes, "I see whatcha mean." She sucked in a deep drag of smoke and spat it out the side of her mouth. She knew.

"I'm gonna head in there now," I said. I was trying to wrap things up. I could see Maxine had finished her call, but instead of joining us, she was sitting at a table, giving us privacy (but still looking curious). "But I wanted someone in your family to know where I went and where Erin might be." I pressed a little slip of paper into her hand. I had drawn a crude map to the bleak house row along the river. "I would say, if you haven't heard from me in twenty-four hours, come in like gangbusters. Tell everyone. The cops. Colin. Everyone. It still might not be too late, but, if we're alive, Erin and I would surely be in deep shit. Can I ask that of you?"

There was a struggle going on behind those fierce blue eyes of hers. After a stuttering pause, she said, "Yeah. I mean, okay. Twenty-four. Yeah." And something snapped. She lost the struggle. "Aw, fuck, Bobber. Fuck dat. I'm comin' with yer!"

I was stunned by her vehemence. My plan was unraveling, and I hadn't even started it yet.

"B-but –" I stammered.

"She's my sister, Bobber! My little sister. You think I can just stand by and wait? Wait for her to be killed? And you too – our sweet, brave, but misguided neighbor boy? Yeah, I get the part about Colin. And the cops. But yer not goin' back to that horrible place alone. I won't let you."

I could see that Maxine's eyes were wide – she still didn't seem able to hear us, but she knew something dramatic was being said. A couple other patrons appeared to be paying attention to us now as well.

"I won't be going in there alone, exactly," I said lamely. I patted my left armpit area. "I'm packin'."

Peggy rolled her eyes again. "You think yer the only one with a gun?" She snapped open her purse. She shoved it under my nose. Under the lipstick tubes and balled up tissue I saw what appeared to be a little Derringer. "Practically everyone in here is armed. So what else is new? So bang-bang. So let's go."

"Peggy, I –"

"Let's go, I already told ya." She trotted over to Maxine and whispered something. I tried to use this as a chance to sneak away. But as I reached the door, she caught up with me and took my arm.

Outside, she whispered, "Let's go get Erin."

I got behind the wheel, and Peggy slid in on the passenger side on the opposite end of the bench seat.

"The old man's DeSoto, huh? I remember hearin' about it, but I'm not sure I ever seed it. Him dyin' so long ago, and all. She's a beauty though." She patted the dashboard as you would the mane of a prize mare.

I put it into gear and we were off. As we headed for Archer, I thought of one more quick stop I wanted to make first. It was still late afternoon and the stores were still open. I was done with that cap, but my head felt naked. I pulled in front of Clancy's Haberdashery and parked.

"I'll only be a minute, Peg. I lost Pa's old hat in the river – I think – and I feel naked without it. Just gonna grab a new lid for myself."

"Sure," said Peggy. "I git yer."

I thought she was going to wait in the car, but Peggy came in with me.

Old Clancy was delighted to see us. Peggy and I had both gone to school with a collection of his own kids.

He pulled the ever-present tape measure from around his neck and measured my melon, whistling at the immensity of it. I winced when the tape pulled against the spot behind my ear where I'd gotten slugged, but I said nothing. He quickly produced an array in my size in browns, grays – and even a black one.

I chose a nice gray felt fedora with a medium band that looked pretty sharp but not show-offy. It had a nice wide brim. In the mirror I almost looked human again. I paid him. Peggy had been digging through a barrel of boys' sneakers over by thc door. She found a pair that fit her pretty well and bought them. We left with our purchases and returned to the car.

As we pulled away, Peggy was lacing up her new sneakers. They were a nice bright white.

"Figured I may as well trade in my heels, as long as I had the opportunity," she said. "Considerin'."

"Yep," I echoed, "considerin'."

We drove in silence for awhile. I was feverishly trying to think of a way to ditch her before we got anywhere dangerous. I thought about stopping somewhere nearby for a bite and calling one of her friends or siblings to come pick her up. But that only seemed like a way to complicate things more.

Finally, as I made the turn from Archer to State, Peg said, "So do we have a plan here, or, what?"

"I confess I do not. We are nearly flying blind. That's why I wanted to go alone."

"Well, ferget that. Yer ain't alone."

"Yep. I know."

"Don't worry We'll get a plan," she said. "One of us will think of somethin'."

That's what I was afraid of.

As the Loop drew ever closer, I said, "There is someplace less dangerous I would like to revisit first. You can come along – it really would be safer for you to be with me than wait in the car."

"Oh, I'm comin' with yer, don't worry about that." Peggy had never left her friendliness and confidence in me behind in her tone. But she did seem to be saying that she wasn't going to take any shit from me, either. So be it.

I just wished that Clancy had also sold boys' pants. Peggy was wearing this very pretty dress with a light blue pattern and little bows here and there – and I hated the thought of her going for a swim in the river in that outfit. It could happen.

We passed the Tribune, and I turned onto Illinois, picked up Rush, and made it back to Hubbard. In the brief time we were on Rush Street, try as I may, I saw no signs advertising a fortune teller or palm reader.

And there was Lana's building. I parked right in front of the out-of-business dry cleaner. We got out, and I made certain to lock the car with all the windows rolled up. A couple of youths loitered down the sidewalk some distance. They didn't look larcenous, but you couldn't bank on good behavior from anyone around here.

"We won't stay here long," I said. "This is where Erin has been living." Peggy's eyes widened as she took in the decrepit neighborhood, but she followed me in through the un-lockable street door.

I led the way, making sure Peggy stayed very close behind me. We ascended the three flights in silence.

When we reached the third floor landing we were aware of muffled talking and strange cooking smells, but we saw no one.

"There's someone I need to talk to first. She's a neighbor and friend of Erin's." I headed for Lana's apartment and Peggy walked alongside me, holding onto my arm. It was my left arm, the one with the wound, but she needed to hold onto something so I let her.

We stood in front of Lana's and I rapped softly on the door. It was very quiet. Sometimes you can knock on someone's door and, if they want to appear not to be home, you can almost tell that they really are by the sudden lack of noise. You can imagine them in there holding perfectly still, hoping you will go away, all squeaks and pops of floorboards ceasing. But there was no such feeling now. I rapped once more. It sounded very, very empty.

"Hmm. She works at a bank," I said. "She's probably still there." I somehow didn't believe it, even as I was speaking the words, but it's what I said.

I looked at Peggy. "No one home, I guess. Would you like to see Erin's place?" I almost said 'where Erin lived' but I resisted the urge to speak of her in the past tense. Peggy grimly nodded her head and I led her across the hall and down to Apartment C.

I had left the door unlocked. But the door had been relocked. Someone had been here. Someone with a key. I rapped on the door. Same empty feeling – I hoped it was empty, anyway, as I intended to break in again.

I took out my cellar door key and did the same thing I had before. This time I got the lock to pop much quicker. I smiled at Peggy and slowly pushed the door open.

"Sweet Jesus," Peg said under her breath, "lookit bloody Jimmy Valentine here." We stepped inside and I shut the door behind us.

Peggy moved slowly around the tiny living/bedroom. She went to the dresser and began pulling open drawers. Peering into one of these, she suddenly leaned over it and began to cry. I led her over to the chair and eased her down onto it.

"Just seein' her things in them drawers. With his. So she was livin' with him. Shacked up with that monkey. No wonder she wouldn't let me visit. I'm sorry –" And she wept a little more. Pulling one of those old tissues from her purse, she dabbed at her eyes. "But ya say, that Picout scum is dead?"

"They fished him out of the lake. That's what the paper said. We'll get out of here in just a second. Let me check out something first." I opened the closet intending to get a look at those cardboard boxes that had been taped up. I was sorry I did.

"Oh, God, her dresses," said Peggy, and she started crying anew. "Lookit them hangin' there. It's so sad."

I did think it was sad. But I was also looking at something else. One of those boxes was gone. "I swear there were two boxes like this here yesterday," I said.

"Somebody must have pinched the other one," said Peggy, blowing her nose as punctuation.

"Let's see what's in this other one," I said. It seemed surprisingly light as I carried it over to the tiny counter next to the sink. I switched on the light bulb, which hung above the kitchenette area, and pulled out my pen knife. It was a matter of moments to slice open the masking tape. I popped open the lid and jumped back with a yelp.

Peggy was on her feet. "What is it?" She cried.

"Sorry. Sorry. I just got surprised. It looks like it's a snake. But it also looks like it might be dead. We need to be careful though."

I began inching back towards it, but Peggy walked right up to the box. "It's dead," she said. "Or wait. What the hell?"

My pride smarting, I approached the box again and peered inside. I understood Peg's confusion. I didn't know what we were looking at. Finally, I took a wooden spoon from a drawer and fished the thing out. I laid it on the counter. It was a dry, crispy looking thing, and it added its own acrid stink to the already reeking apartment. A very long snakeskin, it was the kind shed by living snakes periodically. As kids, we would sometimes find the shed skins of garter snakes in the alleys, in summer. None had ever been this big though.

"Now why was Picout keeping a box with a snakeskin in it?" I asked myself aloud.

"Maybe it was a box with a snakeskin," Peggy said. "Or maybe it used to be a box with a live snake that shed its skin while in there."

As soon as she had said the words, the image of the magazine fer-de-lance came to mind. Both Peggy and I started scanning the floor, looking under the bed, checking all the shadows.

"Come on," I said. I quickly wiped down anything I thought we could have left fingerprints on, and we inched out the door. No one was in the hallway, so I carefully locked it back up with my cellar door key.

"That was damned creepy," said Peggy. "What the hell is Erin involved with?"

"I sure as hell don't know," I said. "Before we go, I want to try Lana's one more time."

We walked back to the door and I rapped once again. Taking out my cellar door key, I said, "I want to check around in there. Just keep a look out. If you hear someone coming, give me a tap on the shoulder, will ya?"

"I'll flatten yer, is more like it. Hurry up, this has got my nerves on edge."

I hurried up. I wasn't sure why exactly, but it suddenly seemed likely we would find that missing cardboard box in Lana's possession.

It took a little more force, but the lock yielded the same way. As I pushed against the door, I waited to see if the chain were engaged. Because if the door were chained, that would mean someone was in there. There was no chain, so we had the place to ourselves. I hurried Peggy in and I shut the door. Remembering the fire escape, I made the loose plan that if we heard the door opening we could slip into the bedroom and out the window, maybe without anyone (Lana, specifically) ever even knowing we'd been there.

"We're looking for the identical mate to that box the snakeskin was in. Try not to touch anything if you can help it; I'll wipe the knobs I've touched. And let's not spend a lot of time."

"Okay," said Peggy, looking on the other side of the loveseat, "if this Lana is Erin's friend, what would she be doing with that other box? Keeping it for her and Vaughn?"

"I don't know, exactly," I said. "I guess I'm just getting the feeling suddenly that maybe Lana isn't really such a good friend of Erin's."

We checked the kitchen and the bathroom and the living room closet. Nothing. I was saving the bedroom for last, mostly because I didn't really want to go back in that particular lair. But I had to see.

"Go wait by the door," I told Peggy. "As soon as I'm done looking in there, we're going to make tracks."

"Right. I'll be glad to get out of here."

I went in. At once I thought I smelled something weird – was it the same smell that snakeskin had? Geez, I thought, I hope that snake isn't crawling around loose in here.

The window was latched, and I unlatched it with my pen knife, just in case. It was still light outside. I looked down at the sidewalk. Lana was not hurrying home.

No box under the bed. No snake, either. Good.

With my hanky, I opened the closet door and switched on the bulb that illuminated it. I stared at the closet floor. Well, I thought, that's where that odor is coming from.

In a sitting up position, slightly sideways so I could see his wrists still tied behind him, covered up partially in several bloody towels and blankets, his throat cut from ear to ear, his eyes open and looking at me plaintively, was my old pal Cappy.

He was very dead.

# Chapter Seven

Peggy and I tried our best to walk at a normal pace down the three flights of steps, but, no denying, there was a real spring in our step. Three regiments of boogeymen nipped at our heels.

I had the doors of the DeSoto unlocked and ourselves seated in it faster than I thought possible. Thank God no one had stolen it.

There was real restraint in my feet as I worked the clutch and gave her gas. I did not want any witness to be able to say that they saw an ancient yellow DeSoto rocketing away from the scene of the crime. How I'd managed to keep a cool enough head to relock Lana's door I will never know.

Peggy hadn't had to look at dead Cappy, as I was out of the bedroom before she could, but she took my word on identity and condition.

"Where are we going?" Peggy wanted to know.

"That's a good question," I said. "We just need somewhere to think this out." And just as I said it, I knew where I wanted to go. I took a right and drove a couple blocks to Grand Avenue. Once there, I relocated Millie's Soda Fountain where Birdie worked. It had only been about twenty-four hours since I'd first been there, but it seemed a lifetime ago.

"What's here?" Peggy asked.

"Food, coffee – and a place to collect our brains for a second."

"Sounds good, let's go."

Inside, it was exactly the same as before. Birdie was working on neatening up the newsstand again. When she saw me she smiled and walked over, pulling her pencil out of her hair.

I introduced she and Peggy, and the two eyed each other, not unfriendly, but not terribly friendly either.

"Whatja do to yer eye?" asked Birdie. "Started boxing again?"

I chuckled. "Something like that." She took our orders. I ordered a burger and coffee, and Peggy went with the grilled cheese with tomato, and a coke.

When she left, Peggy said, "I think she likes you. And she doesn't like me at all." She didn't say it like it bothered her, but like a sociologist might say it, lecturing a college class.

"Everybody likes me till they get to know me," I said, not knowing what else to say. Thankfully, Peggy let the subject drop.

While we waited for our food, I got up and walked around.  I knew Peggy and I had a lot we should be discussing, but my brain was turned inside out.

Peggy walked over to the booth and made a call.  I really hoped she wasn't blabbing to her family, but there wasn't a Goddamned thing I could do about it.

They had small bottles of aspirin for sale and I grabbed one up.  My wound was throbbing again and I intended to take several with my coffee. Looking beyond the aspirin aisle, I saw a display of photographic-type equipment arranged in the far corner of the store.  I strolled over to it.  This brought me close to the druggist working behind the counter.  He looked up at me with a wary smile.

"How's it goin'" I asked him.

"Just fine.  Let me know if you need any help."

"Will do, Chief, thanks."

When I got to the display, I realized it was a lot of optical odds and ends, reading glasses, magnifying glasses, stuff like that.

On the bottom shelf – out of my line of sight from the aspirin area – was a dusty old pair of binoculars. They gave me an idea. I picked them up and looked them over. There was no price tag. I brought them over to the druggist.

"How much for the binocs?" I asked. "I don't see a price."

He took them from me and blew some dust off them with a chuckle. Looking them over he said, "The old field glasses? Damn, I think I forgot they were even over there. Put 'em out more for display. They've probably sat there for close to a decade. Guy short on cash brought them in one day to help settle a bill. I took them, but never saw him again."

"Are they for sale?"

"I guess so. Never had a price on them. You wanna buy 'em?"

"I guess so. How much you want?"

"What you want to offer me?"

"I don't know," I said. "How 'bout five bucks?"

"A fin? Sold."

I dug out five ones and he forked over the binoculars.

"Do they work?" I asked.

"I don't know," said the druggist. He was a big jolly guy and he reminded me a lot of the actor Jack Carson, only with blonder, thinning hair. "You want a bag?"

I raised them to my eyes, there were no caps on the lenses. They were pretty dirty.

The druggist handed me a tissue and I gave the eyepieces a good wipe. Raising them to my eyes again, I worked the focus wheel until I had a view of Birdie, enlarged and crisp and clear. She looked over at me and waggled her fingers.

"They work," I said. "I don't need a bag. Thanks, Chief."

I walked back to the lunch counter. Birdie disappeared to check on the food just as Peggy returned from her phone call.

"What's with those things?" Peggy asked.

"I just bought 'em. I don't know. They might come in handy, I thought."

"Yeah, if yer goin' inta the Peepin' Tom business." We both laughed, but it was forced. Nothing seemed very funny at the moment.

"Who did you call?" I asked.

"Maxine. I tried Tim's first, but she'd left. I caught her at her mom's house. I'd told her I was goin' into town with yer, but I didn't explain why – don't worry, I didn't give away what we're up to. But I know she knows it's about Erin. Just now, I asked if she could please lie for me and call my folks. I told her to tell them I went dancin' with yer. They'll know I'm safe if yer with me." I hoped that was true. "Even if they don't believe the dancin' part. I just didn't want to get on the phone with my mother. It's too hard."

Just then, Birdie brought out our plates. We settled down and ate. I couldn't believe I would ever be hungry again after getting a look at Cappy in the closet. But I was voracious.

We tucked away in silence, and Birdie refreshed our drinks. Then Peggy said with a mouthful of food, "So – what's it all mean, Bobber? Does it mean this Lana killed that guy? And what do they have to do with Erin?"

"I don't know," I said. "I really don't know. I guess Lana must have killed him – unless somebody was hiding in her apartment when she told me he'd gotten away. Maybe he killed Cappy – and after I'd left he killed Lana too. Maybe that's why she wasn't home."

I'd told Peggy that after I'd been attacked on the street, I'd returned to Lana's for help, and she had stitched me up. I said shortly after that, Cappy snuck in the window and attacked us, but I had subdued and tied him up – and that I'd seen his partner on the landing and given chase. Which was how I'd ended up in the river. I said nothing about my excursion into Lana's bed, and didn't intend to unless pushed to the wall over it. Luckily, Peggy didn't pursue that angle.

"I don't like it, Bobber. People getting' killed. Dead bodies in closets. Snakes! We've got to find Erin."

I wanted to say "we will" but bit my tongue.

"I think we need to get into that house down on the river. I'm just not sure how to do it without endangering her," is what I said instead.

Peggy asked Birdie if they had a ladies' room in "this dump," and Birdie directed her through the same doors that led to their little kitchen.

Peggy excused herself and I motioned Birdie over. I had an idea while we were eating. It was a good idea, I thought. And I needed to act quickly or I might blow my one opportunity.

As Birdie listened, I explained that Peggy was the sister of that neighbor I had originally asked about and that she, Erin, was missing. I briefly explained to Birdie what I intended to do – and could she please explain all this to my new pal the druggist, and of course Peggy. I warned her that Peggy was going to hate the idea, but to be persistent. Birdie seemed to understand, and I fled the scene.

The DeSoto started and it pulled from the curb. I looked in the rearview mirror just in time to see Peggy burst from the building in a rage, with Birdie close on her heels, yakking a blue streak. I could just hear Peggy yelling, "What a lousy trick!" before I turned the corner.

It was a lousy trick. But it had to be done.

## Chapter Eight

The sign on Millie's Soda Fountain glass door said they were open till midnight, eight p.m. on Sundays – only it was far from being Sunday. What needed doing could be done well before midnight and it was only a little after five right now.

I had given Birdie the super edited version of the situation: Peggy's sister was in great danger. I had an idea to save her, but I had to do it alone. I wanted Peggy to wait for me at the drugstore. I wouldn't be longer than two or three hours. In that time, I would come back with or without Erin, but, either way, Peggy could go with me wherever she wanted afterwards. But this part I had to do alone.

What I avoided saying was if I got killed I didn't want Peggy to also get killed.

I hoped if Birdie told her employer, the druggist that looked lke Jack Carson, together they might calm Peggy down and make her listen to reason. If the druggist would even want to get involved. That was a gamble. And with what I saw in the rearview mirror, they would have their work cut out for them. The only way for me to avoid Peg's wrath was to bring back Erin.

I looked at my new/old field glasses I had just purchased – lying on the seat next to me. I hoped they would do me some good. But first I needed to do one more thing.

Between Illinois Street and the river, Rush Street only runs for a couple longish blocks. I parked at the corner of Illinois and Rush and got out, locking the binoculars in the car. I intended walking up and down that two block stretch looking for any sign of that fortune teller's storefront Maeve had visited. If this were the location of that fortune teller's storefront, its proximity to that river house was too outlandish to be a coincidence.

Things were still pretty quiet here, but I knew it would soon be bustling. Rush had a collection of taverns and stores that stayed open late, and while I hadn't been down in this area much, I'd heard stories about it. It was definitely a place where you could do things that decent folk probably didn't know existed. After dark, it transformed into what the righteous might describe as a Den of Sin. But in the daylight, it was still a place where you could buy a bag of groceries in relative safety. Or a pair of shoes.

And there across the street I saw a shoe store sign. I crossed in the middle of the block, keeping an eye out for a cop who might be in the mood to nail a jaywalker (but down here, that probably never happened). The store was locked tight, but that didn't matter. I took a little walk one way and really saw nothing that could even pretend to be a fortune teller's. Before I'd even reached the end of the block, I turned around and decided to try the other side of the shoe store. This plan yielded rewards almost at once.

Only a couple buildings down from the shoe store, there was what appeared to be a vacant building. But on closer inspection, the big window that faced the street displayed a small hand-painted sign, no more than three feet by two feet – hardly visible to a passing vehicle – that read: FORTUNES TOLD.

I immediately backed away and returned to the closed shoe store. There was a recessed doorway, and I stepped into it, trying to look like I was checking out the window displays while waiting to meet someone – but mostly trying to keep out of the line of sight of anyone coming out the door of the Fortune Teller's building.

Taking furtive peeks at that deserted-looking establishment, it did not take long for me to spot someone emerging from it.

I was first aware of the sound of a door opening and the jangle of jewelry. She was not visible to me at first, but I soon caught glimpses of a tallish woman with long gray hair protruding from under a silky turban. She wore huge gypsy-like hoop earrings, and a multitude of bracelets from both wrists. Her fingers, as well, were adorned with flashy rings. She appeared to be studying the foot traffic on Rush, as she slowly raised a cigarette to her lips, puffing thoughtfully (that smoke reached my nostrils, carried on the wind). I ducked out of sight when her gaze began to turn my direction.

Here was Maeve's palm reader, I was sure of it. She slowly surveyed the street a couple more times, languidly enjoying that smoke, then I heard her go back inside. I ran to the corner (the one in the direction that would not take me past her storefront), crossed the street, and got in the DeSoto. I could still see her shop from there though I was farther away. I casually and gently set the binoculars on my lap.

By now it was getting pretty dark. Making certain that no one was watching me, I slowly raised the binoculars to my eyes and focused. Almost at once, I got a magnified image of the fortune teller leaving and locking up her shop. She was alone.

I watched carefully to see if she got into a parked car nearby. But she didn't. She headed south along the sidewalk and continued that direction.

I started the engine and slowly followed her, pulling into a new parking spot, periodically, then resuming. As often as I could, I raised the binoculars to my eyes. I wanted to get a good look at her face so I might identify her without her gypsy get-up. But so far a good look at her remained elusive.

The more she walked, however, the more obvious her goal. It had to be that house on the river.

On an impulse, I made a quick right at the next side street. Driving away from Rush, I went around the next block and headed toward the river

– and that house – trying to beat the fortune teller there.

I was about half a block from the house when I parked, shut off the lights and turned off the engine. Like clockwork, I saw the fortune teller come around the corner and head for the house – and in my direction. I raised the binoculars to my eyes and finally got a good look at her face in the glow of the streetlight.

Lana.

She was wearing a long gray wig that stuck out from under her turban. But there was no mistaking the cast of that face.

I watched as she approached the house in question. She went up to a nondescript door on the side facing me. Rather than knock, she produced a set of keys, unlocked the door, and entered – slamming the door shut behind her.

So, what the hell was going on here? I had to sit and collect my thoughts, and they were scattered.

A furious banging on the window next to my head shattered my reverie. The binoculars flew out of my hands.

My head snapped to the left – and there was the angry face of Peg O'Kief.

"What the hell, Bobber?" Peg screamed. "How dare you try and ditch me with a dirty trick like that?"

"Get in the car and stop that noise!" was all I could think to yell in return. Peg circled the DeSoto like a demon and was sitting next to me the next instant. She was gulping air – her eyes and hair wild.

Before she could sputter another word, I said, "How the hell did you find me?"

"Yer little waitress girlfriend," she spat – and even as she said it, I saw another car making a hasty retreat in the direction I had come. "I told her she better help me find you and pronto or I'd teach her some tricks on that hamburger griddle."

"For Christ's sake, Peg! I was coming back for you!"

Peg was spitting and stammering – clearly too angry to form words, so I jumped back into it. "Peg, look. Erin may still be alive, but one wrong step might get her killed. We have to be careful. I'm not about to go to your poor parents and tell them I've gotten two of their daughters killed."

This remark had the desired result, but she still didn't seem too pleased with me.

"All right, Bobber," she said, breathing heavily, trying to subdue her temper. "I see your point. But I still ain't goin' nowhere. So what's goin' on? What are we gonna do?

I filled her in on more details about the house and my disastrous and very wet first visit. I also got her up-to-date on Lana, and how it looked like she was really this Madame Hilda – Erin's employer and maybe even her captor. I just finished telling her about my having seen Lana let herself into the place with a key, when we both spotted another figure approaching the house.

He came from the direction of Rush Street, same as Lana, and he may have been one of her henchmen – staying behind at the storefront to finish some clean-up business, maybe, and now rejoining her. The guy was a monster. In fact, in stature he resembled Frankenstein's monster. Hired muscle, for sure. And the shape of the monster looked familiar. I was almost certain he had been one of the guys who had tried to drown me.

I put the binoculars to my eyes and studied him.

He approached the door Lana had used, but instead of using a key, he raised a prime rib-sized fist and rapped on the door with his knuckles, backhanded. A small panel on the door opened and shut quickly. Then the whole door opened and the monster gained entrance. I could not tell who it was that let in the beast.

"Who the hell was that?" Peg asked.

"I don't know. Maybe the butler."

"Yer such an asshole." Then in a much tinier voice, she added, "I can't bear the thought of Erin being in the hands of those monkeys, Bobber."

"I know, Peg. Neither can I."

"So what do we do?"

"I tell you what," I said with a resolve that I really didn't completely feel, "let's make a plan."

It wasn't much of a plan, but it was all we had. I would attempt to enter the house by the same door we had just seen Big Boy enter. If I were successful, Peg would wait an hour, not a minute more, and she would run and get the cops. I told her to make up any story she could think of. I warned her about the DeSoto's old clutch, but she assured me she would have no trouble driving the car. In the meantime, she would lie low and, with the help of the binoculars, keep an eye on the place. I told her I would trust her judgment if she felt she needed to get the cops early.

"And what are you gonna be doing exactly?" she asked.

"If Erin is really in there, I'm going to try to get her out of there."

I handed the car keys to Peg and opened the driver's door. Before I could get out, however, she grabbed my wrist, leaned over, and kissed my cheek.

"Hey, don't die, okay?" she whispered.

"I'll do my best," I said, and left the car. I caught a fleeting glimpse of Peg scooting behind the steering wheel as I headed down the street.

# Chapter Nine

Some walks seem to take forever when you are excited about the destination. Every time my friends and I, as kids, had walked to Comiskey Park it seemed an eternity. My walk to the big scary house this night, however, seemed as though I had been shot from a cannon. It was just as well – there was a chilly, stinky wind blowing off the river and I only wore my suit jacket and hat for protection.

Once at the door, I could hear a radio playing. I swallowed my spit and knocked as if I belonged there.

The little door within the door opened and a beady pair of eyes looked at me suspiciously. "What do you want?" asked the voice that belonged to the eyes.

"I've got your comic books," I heard myself saying. I had not planned to say it – it just came out of my mouth.

"Comic books?" asked the voice.

"Sure. One load of 'Archie,' and a whole box full of 'Casper the Friendly Ghost.'"

"Casper?"

"The friendliest ghost you know. Come on, I got a ton of deliveries to finish tonight. You want 'em or not?"

"Let me see those things." And the door flew open.

I didn't wait for any further comic book chit chat. I yanked the guy out by the arms and landed an uppercut right on the tip of his chin – the sweet spot. He went down like cooked noodles.

The very ncxt thing I did was poke my head inside. He had been alone in this room which looked like a kitchen. No sign of Big Boy. Good. The coast was clear, for the moment. Entering, I found little I might use to tie up the guy I had just laid low, except a few short electrical cords. Before settling on these, I looked outside again and saw an old garden hose coiled up by the side of the house. Using my pen knife, I managed to cut the hose into a few sections and these worked well enough to tie the guy up by the ankles and wrists. He had begun moaning just as I was finishing. There was a pile of rags near the hose, and I cut a few strips from these, stuffing a wad into his mouth very tightly and using another strip to secure the wad in his mouth, gag-style. I then carried him like a sack of laundry (he wasn't very big) and tied him with another hunk of hose to a fence post behind some trash cans. I looked him over, inspecting my work. He might eventually be able to wriggle out of the brittle hose parts, but it would take him awhile. His eyes started blinking and he looked up at me angrily, so I tapped him on the chin again (this time about twice as hard) sending him to a happier place for a period of time. I hoped it would be long enough.

I looked up the street and could barely make out the light color of the DeSoto. I could not tell if Peg were watching, but I waggled my fingers briefly in her direction, stepped back inside, and quietly shut the door behind me – making sure to leave it unlocked.

The radio was still playing and I left it alone. It was good cover. There was an open doorway in the rear wall, revealing a dark hallway. In this, I could see the dim outline of stairs going up. I could hear no other sounds but those coming from the radio.

I drew the Colt from the holster and stepped into the hall.

Now I was aware of the faintest echo of a human talking, but, with the radio also playing, I could not tell if the voice were even male or female. It did seem to be coming from somewhere on the same floor.

I decided to try my luck upstairs. Ascending carefully and slowly, trying not to make the wooden steps creak, I rose into the darkness like a gun-toting snail.

As I reached the landing and made the turn, I could see three doors, all open a crack, all spilling meager pools of light into a tiny hall. It looked as though the stairs continued up at least to one more floor. Before I even reached this floor with the three doors, however, I became aware of sounds issuing from the nearest doorway.

I stood very still, listening. A male voice was saying things. But it was not a conversation. They were low, sporadic mutterings as though the guy were talking to himself under his breath.

I waited and listened some more for a couple minutes. The quiet monologue continued, and it did not appear as though my approach had been detected by this mutterer.

Hugging the side of the steps next to the railing, I continued all the way up.

I peeked into that first open door and was somewhat stunned to see a familiar face. It was Blaine, the autograph hound from the café where

Lana and I had eaten dinner the night before. He was supposed to be a big fan of mine. But suddenly, I was not sure how much I should believe that.

Blaine was the disgruntled mutterer I'd been hearing, which he continued to be as I watched. He wore a giant pair of leather gloves (almost like those gauntlets worn by falconers) and with good reason. The room contained fifty or so glass terrariums strewn about on tabletops, shelves, and even the floor. And each of these contained one or more snakes. And each of these snakes – that ranged from black to brown to tan colored – seemed to have a double row of a triangle-like pattern along its back. Many of them had yellow chins. And all bore a chilling resemblance to the snake in the torn-out magazine page I had found in Vaughn and Erin's apartment. The fer-de-lance.

And my old buddy Blaine appeared to be going from pen to pen checking the snakes. But what he didn't appear to be was happy about his job.

Quietly, gun still drawn, I stepped into the room. I waited for him to see me first. And when he did, he couldn't have looked more surprised.

"Yeah, that's right," I said in a low voice, "it's me. Hands in the air."

He stuck those big leather gloves above his head. He looked quite foolish.

"So, how is that autograph working out? Got it framed yet?" I asked. To be honest, I wasn't quite sure what I was going to do, now that I had the drop on him. Should I just comb the building, I thought, knocking out and tying up guys? Maybe, I also thought. But before it came to that, he spoke.

"N-no," he stammered, "that was real. I mean, I was working for Madame Hilda when I introduced myself, but I really wanted that autograph. I am a big fan."

"Is that so?"

"Yeah. I've got it in my shirt pocket here. I've been showing it to everyone. You want me to show you?"

"Just keep yer hands in the air for now."

His confused expression suddenly contorted with further confusion.

"Wait. Do you want it back or somethin'? Is that what this is about?"

"No, I want a buck. Those things ain't free, you know." Before he started digging for his wallet (or a switchblade, maybe), I said, "I'm just kidding. That's not why I'm here." I wanted to add 'you idiot' – but, as Ma always says, you catch more flies with honey, if you want some God-damned flies so bad. Instead, I told him quite simply that I was looking for a redheaded girl named Erin, and I believed she was in this building somewhere.

Without hesitating, old Blaine said, "I know the girl you mean. I know Erin, I like her, she's nice. If you want to take her out of here, I can try to help you. She doesn't belong here."

I let him talk. Eventually I let him lower his hands though I kept the Colt in my grip. Even if I could trust Blaine (and I didn't know yet if I could), I had no idea who might come popping in on us.

Blaine was supposed to have met Lana (known to him and the others as "Hilda") at the café last night and then he was to have escorted her home. When I had walked in with her, she made eye contact with him and motioned that he was free to take off since she had me as protection back to her place. But he had recognized me, and, waiting for her to go to the bathroom, he had come over to introduce himself the way he did, risking her possible wrath when she returned and saw us talking.

"I haven't spoken to her since. I know she's here somewhere in the house. But it's a big building. So I don't know if she's angry or not."

It turned out that he was a member of a growing number of her inner circle who were becoming disillusioned with serving in her army of crime. He had to be careful. Vaughn Picout had defied her and he had ended up dead – and his girlfriend Erin had been enslaved in Hilda's prostitution ring.

I asked if Cappy had been a friend of his. He said yes. Then I took on the grim responsibility of telling him his friend had been murdered – probably by Hilda herself.

Poor Blaine's expression darkened. He was quiet for a moment or two, then he practically whispered: "Like I told you, I can help you get Erin out of here."

Before we did anything else, though, I tried to get as much information out of him as possible. He didn't know the answers to all my questions, but he knew a lot.

For instance, he knew that Lana/Hilda, in fact, had been an Army nurse, a captain in the WACs. She'd been stationed in an American camp in Central America – in Honduras, to be precise.

Sometime during the early years of the war, she'd gotten herself dishonorably discharged. Blaine didn't know the details, but Lana, when she did allude to it, laughed about it as if it were a joke. Her unit had been scheduled to ship out to the Pacific somewhere, and she got to miss all the fun.

"But before she left Honduras, she learned her big secret." And it was this secret that helped form what she became. And it explained this room full of highly poisonous fer-de-lances. From somewhere in the hidden side of the native Honduran population, Hilda had learned a particularly powerful form of mind control over someone, using a combination of hypnosis and extremely fresh venom from the fer-de-lance.

"I only just met her yesterday" I told him at last, "and she said her name was Lana, not Hilda."

"Yeah," said Blaine, "I know she uses that name too, but I don't think it's her real name either. I don't think anyone around here knows her real name. I'm only one of a few who knows she puts on that gypsy accent. Or wears a gray wig."

"So, what is this power she has over people?"

Blaine swallowed hard unintentionally. "Well, have you ever heard of zombies?"

I'd heard of them but I didn't know much about them. "That's some voodoo shit, right? From, like, Haiti? People walking like The Mummy, mental slaves of other people, being forced to work on plantations? I always thought it was the bunk – except in the movies."

"No bunk," said Blaine. "Not at all. You're looking at a zombie, man. At least now I'm a former zombie. I hope." I hoped so too – for my own sake, for Erin's sake.

According to Blaine, there were zombies (he also had a couple other names for them) throughout the Caribbean Islands and in South America and Central America, as well. Hilda had connected with a particularly vicious zombie cult while in Honduras. They were her kind of people. And a properly created zombie didn't shuffle around, staring blankly, and muttering "yes, Master," either. A properly created zombie appeared very much like the person appeared before. Only now they behaved like a slave, showing an extraordinary fear of disobeying the person who had transformed them.

And the venom of the fer-de-lance from Honduras was particularly good at achieving this effect.

"You become a zombie in three steps," said Blaine. "You are hypnotized (Hilda is very good at that part). Then you get injected with or drink her serum – this stuff she makes herself, nobody knows what's in it. It also acts as a kind of anti-venom, because the third step is you drink or are injected with venom. The fresher the better, and injection works best. There's also a quick way to do it, but it involves letting the snake bite the person directly. And, I have to say, I've seen the bite method almost never work."

Shortly after getting kicked out of the service, Hilda arrived in Chicago with her newly acquired secret and a dream in tow.

She started out as the storefront palm reader/fortune teller. It didn't take long for her to attract a core group of guys around her.

"I was not part of that group," said Blaine, "I came within her first year, though. She started out with one fer-de-lance that she had managed to smuggle out of Honduras. She wanted to get more – maybe raise them herself. She advertised for someone who knew a lot about snakes, for someone who was interested in working with them. I was just out of high school and was planning to study snakes and lizards, herpetology, in college.

But I saw that ad, and – well my plans kinds got derailed."

What Hilda had envisioned (at least what she told her new minions) was a vast criminal empire based in Chicago. She planned to traffic in anything above, below, and beyond the law —from narcotics to money laundering and everything in between. Things had begun promisingly enough, but since her mind control methods needed repeating every two to three weeks, much of her time began to get used up keeping her people under her spell. The last couple years, the whole thing seemed to deteriorate into an opium den and a brothel.

"Women who feel the need to sell themselves, for whatever the reason, tend to hook up with genuine pimps or else they simply freelance – and they steer clear of Hilda and her methods. These days she uses that fortune teller business mostly as a way to recruit – really kidnap – girls into the whorehouse here. That's why a woman with Erin's natural attributes is so valuable to Hilda."

This last comment made me nauseous and I almost pasted good old Blaine in the teeth for even saying it. But I kept my head, hoping he really could help me. I saw now that Maeve really had dodged a bullet!

"Just one more thing," I said. "What do you mean by you were a zombie, and now you hope you're not? Just what is this hold she has over people like? Why can't you just shake it off, do whatever you damn want?"

For the first time since this conversation began, Blaine looked downright ashamed of himself. He sighed before he spoke next.

"That's a very difficult and complicated question to answer."

"Do your best."

"Okay. Well, it's nightmarish, for starts, I've never known such fear before. With her method, during the hypnosis, you are given a sense that to disobey her is to suffer horribly. Even to think about disobeying her will do it. It's so hard to describe, but it feels like a white hot fire is bursting from your spine and brain, consuming you as if you were in Hell. It is very real. Very terrifying. I mean, there's more to it than that. But that's the best I can describe it."

"So, how is it that you are escaping her control? Are you really?" Suddenly, I was having further doubts about Blaine's sincerity. I would really have to watch him.

A few months ago, before their regular "booster treatment" by Lana, a small group of them began to talk, compare notes. The group included Blaine, Vaughn Picout, Cappy, and a couple others. They all had left their former lives behind and were now living either in this house or near Lana's apartment. (I noted, too, that the late Vaughn Picout had been living across the hall from her.) And, to a man, they all hated this new existence. And they all hated living with this nightmarish fear.

"Even having this first conversation, we all experienced symptoms, breaking out in cold sweats, etcetera. We learned pretty damn quick that if we were going to talk about it, we would have to refer to things, situations, very indirectly or it would mean disaster. But also, well, this has everything to do with the difference between her male and female zombies."

It was very weird to hear him use the word 'zombies' in such a serious, matter-of-fact way.

"What difference do you mean?" I asked.

"I've gotta watch it," he said, glancing briefly at the floor, "even now – I feel as though any moment I;m going to be down on my knees throwing up, sick to my stomach. Just from talking about this. But it's okay. Yeah, it seems okay. What we're talking about here is sex."

"Sex?"

"Yeah. Um, see… part of her process of control is, well, she has sex with the person she's transforming. Just the once. The first time. But it makes it like you fall in love with her, in a kind of very sick, twisted way. So you feel this sick, painful despair at the thought of, well, losing her. She only had sex with me that first time. Just like with all the others. But I'm still feeling afraid of it, still getting over it." He shook his head and shivered slightly.

This was getting to be too much – especially considering what I'd been through with her my own self. The stitches in my arm tingled distractingly.

"So the zombies she makes with women are…"

"They're not the same, that's for sure," said Blaine, shivering a little once more. "I've seen her do the whole bit with women, including the sex part. Seen it work. But in those cases, they were women who already liked women. Hilda seems like she can have sex with anyone – male or female – but, personally, I don't think she really likes either gender over the other. With her, sex is just another way to get power."

"So Erin is…"

"No, she never had sex with Erin. Like most of Hilda's 'girls' who live as prisoners here, she is much more the drugged-up and hypnotized variety of zombie."

"And Hilda has customers who will pay to be with – a zombie?" It was difficult to hide my utter astonishment.

"Oh, yeah," Blaine said, a bit surprised that I could be so naïve, "they come here looking for exactly that. They're not a whole lot of them, but they help keep the place in groceries."

I'd had just about enough of this. Before I grabbed Blaine by his neck and broke it, I said, "Well, let's get Erin out of here. Enough palaver."

"Okay, we'll get her, but listen, okay?" he said raising his gloved hands defensively.

"Yeah?"

"I'm agreeing to help Erin. But understand – I'm still struggling to keep my head above water. My friends and I –" he paused, probably remembering that some of those friends were now dead, "we've been helping each other by switching our injections with plain saline. That's how our minds have cleared. But if I ever tried to run for it, Hilda would send someone, probably that big ape Slag, to kill me. She's done it before. She thinks nothing of killing people. She's ruthless. So – "

"So?"

"So if we get caught, I'll still try to help you, but I might have to pretend I'm still under her control. Understand?"

"I understand," I said. "Let's go."

Blaine removed his big leather gloves and laid them on the edge of one of the long wooden tables, next to a terrarium. As he did so, the occupant of the terrarium lunged at Blaine's bare hand on the other side of the glass, thrusting its head with alarming speed, and making a loud *thunk* sound against the glass. The sound echoed throughout the room. Blaine ignored the whole thing as if this were all in a day's work. As for myself, I could barely keep from jumping into the air to hang from a ceiling fixture – and I had fought Nazis in hand-to-hand combat. I was glad to be leaving this room that not only held more poisonous snakes than one normally sees in

Illinois, but also smelled like Satan's forgotten gym bag.

Blaine walked to a door opposite the one I had entered. He quietly opened it and stuck his head into the dimness beyond, looking for company. Finding none, he waved me on as he left the room. I followed him stealthily, my gun still drawn. I wasn't exactly holding it on Blaine anymore, but I wasn't exactly not holding it on him either.

Despite the chilly wind outside, it was hot as hell in this building. Blaine wore a short sleeved bowling type shirt (the kind Peg had described being worn by Vaughn Picout), and he looked cool as a mackerel in it. But under my jacket, the rivulets of perspiration had begun to flow down my sides. I didn't know how they could stand it in here. Maybe they had the heat cranked up because of their precious reptiles. Besides the hiss of snakes, I thought I could detect the hiss of radiators as well. This place did not have the welfare of humans as its priority..

Blaine made his way to the foot of a stairway going up, different from the flight I had seen. He peered up into the darkness and listened a moment. Then he motioned for me to follow. I did.

As we got closer to the next floor (the third, if I were counting correctly), a different sound replaced the hissing of reptiles and radiators. This was the whirring of electric fans. But almost at once I heard another sound too. The quiet weeping of female voices.

Before we reached the top, Blaine stopped on the steps and looked at me. In the poor light, I could just barely make out that he was pointing up the stairs and silently mouthing the words, "She's up here."

Trying to grip the Colt more lightly so it wouldn't go off in my hand (the safety was not engaged), I followed Blaine the rest of the way up.

Even in the darkness, I could see the ever-present peeling green paint with lath sticking out here and there. Once upon a time, this building must have housed some kind of modest factory surrounded by little offices and store rooms. The present occupants seemed to be doing nothing towards its upkeep, just like a bunch of river rats that had moved in (and these were probably there as well, hiding behind the lath and crumbling plaster). This next floor was a converted attic with a ceiling that sloped to each side with a narrow floor running between facing rows of skinnier-than-normal doors. There was an open window at each end of this hall. And each of the doors stood slightly ajar, all but two of these had a wooden chair with a small electric fan facing into its very own room. These were the fans I'd heard up here, and they couldn't be doing much good in the stifling heat. Across each of the windows on either end of the hall was fixed a set of iron bars. No one would be escaping easily from the attic tonight.

We reached the nearest door. Blaine turned off the little motor that spun the pathetic blade and he slid the chair and fan out of the way. He stepped into the room with me peering over his shoulder.

The space appeared to be a longish broom closet lit by a bare bulb hanging above our heads. There was no window, and the hot air that the little fan had been moving around was suffocating. It also smelled of human feces and urine. The room was divided in half by a door of makeshift bars someone had fashioned from conduit pipe. This barred door was screwed into the left hand wall with hinges and secured to the right hand wall with a padlock, thus creating a pocket-sized jail cell inside the broom closet. I imagined all the rooms up here were similarly outfitted. Inside this cell, along the back wall, were a couple of large metal buckets, and next to these was a wooden stool on which sat a metal water pitcher and a dirty glass with an even dirtier toothbrush and a bar of soap lying next to that. A collection of gray, moldy towels were stuffed under the stool. This vile little "bathroom" explained the smell. On the floor nearest the cell door sat a tray with unfinished bread crusts on it and a plate smeared with a brown, gravy-like substance. A couple of flies buzzed about this mess risking their lives. Next to the plate was a coffee cup with about an inch of cold coffee still sitting in it. There was a chair with several dresses draped over it, and next to that an open fruit crate that held various undergarments.

And in the middle of this cell, shoved against the wall, was a cot with a pile of bedclothes and a pillow, all in disarray. And on the bedding lay a woman, quietly crying.

It was Erin.

# Chapter Ten

As soon as I realized who it was I was seeing, I rushed to the padlock and jammed the barrel of the Colt against it, ready to blow it to smithereens. Blaine staid my hand.

"No!" he said in a hoarse, loud whisper. "That'll bring them running for sure. I can unlock these." And he produced a jingling key ring.

"Erin!" I whispered as forcefully as I could. "Erin! It's Bobber. From the neighborhood. I'm getting you out of here!"

The pathetic little figure on the cot silenced herself and groggily raised her head off the pillow. Her red hair was plastered to her forehead by sweat.

She looked at her visitors in genuine confusion and finally said, "Bobber? Bobber Maxwell? What are..." She sounded drunk.

Blaine got the padlock off and he swung the door open. I was about to run in, but I motioned with the Colt that I wanted Blaine to precede me. He entered showing he understood my hesitation. But I was right behind him.

Erin was only wearing a sweat-soaked slip. I gently put my free hand under her right arm and motioned to Blaine to help get her standing. He lifted under her left arm and said, "Careful. She's going to be woozy for a while. Really woozy."

We slowly dragged her off the cot and for a moment her legs remained curled under her and a foot or so off the floor as if they didn't realize they weren't in bed anymore. But then they slowly lowered. She was very unsteady.

"Erin, do you think you can stand?" I said. "Can you walk at all?"

"Bobber, what…"

"She'll be able to walk soon," said Blaine, "as soon as she realizes it's expected of her." Blaine was helping, but I hated the way he had of talking about Erin – as if she wasn't right there with us. Unfortunately, I still needed his help.

"We're going to start walking now, Erin, okay?" I said.

"Okay," she slurred, still drunk on fer-de-lance venom, still unsure of what was happening.

Blaine and I now each slung one of her arms around our necks and, everybody taking baby steps, we moved her out of her cell and then out into the hall.

"Where to now?" I asked Blaine. "The way we came?"

I motioned with my head towards the stairs. Blaine never had the chance to answer because just then, looking shocked as hell, I saw there was another guy paused at the top of the landing and blinking. Like the late Cappy, this kid was also Asian and looked barely out of his teens.

"Look out, he's got a gun," said Blaine, turning his best turncoat on me, just as he had promised. "Do as he says."

"That's right," I agreed, motioning with the Colt while still supporting Erin. "Come over here and lie face down on the floor."

Hesitantly, the kid came nearer and made a move to get on the floor. But suddenly, he lunged at me and I saw he carried a blackjack. The weapon clipped me in my right temple, but I had moved out of the way just in time to avoid more serious contact. I dropped the Colt on the floor and brought my right fist up into his bread basket. Blaine took Erin's full weight as we heard the air whoosh out of his lungs with a grunt, and then I smashed him in the face with a left hook. Messy but effective. He hit the wall and slid into a heap, unaware that he was blowing blood bubbles from his nose in his sleep. I picked the Colt up off the floor and took hold of Erin again.

"Can you get him tied up and gagged and lock him in Erin's cell somehow?" I asked Blaine.

"I can try," said Blaine.

"Do it quickly," I said. "We'll wait here."

"What did you do to Sam?" Erin asked.

"Just teaching him to cover his nose when he sneezes. Don't worry about it."

I saw Blaine pocket Sam's dropped blackjack. He then had just begun to drag the unconscious man back into Erin's room when we were surprised by two more guys.

"Watch out, he's got a gun!" Blaine said again. I was getting pretty sick of it.

They must have heard the scuffle with Sam from downstairs because these two came rushing at me without hesitation. Taking Blaine's advice and not wanting my fired gun bringing even more of these rats down on us, I holstered the Colt just as one of the guys went to pull Erin out of my grip, and the other was going right after my head with a ball bat.

Erin screamed.

I yanked the bat out of the guy's grip and shoved it into his stomach, shutting him up momentarily. The other guy, in fact, had pulled Erin out of my grip as I played baseball with his friend.  But as soon as I had control of the bat, I swung it at the guy holding Erin and caught him in the small of the back.  He collapsed on the floor whimpering.  I grabbed up Erin before she hit the floor as well.

"No time to tie anyone up," I said to Blaine, "let's move!"

But before we were blessed with movement, a giant head appeared coming up the stairs.  It was the guy Blaine had referred to as Slag, the very same monster Peg and I had seen entering the building from afar.  Up close, he was even more gruesome.  He had yellow eyes decorated with red spider webs.  His head did seem square like Karloff's in the old movies.  And as his body followed his head up the steps, it wasn't clear if he was muscle gone to fat or just fat.  It didn't matter.  He was doing a volume business.  And, as he grinned, he didn't seem worried about my presence at all.

I pulled the Colt, not caring how much noise I made now.

"Watch out, Slag," I heard Blaine say, "he's got a gun!"

I aimed and squeezed the trigger – at least I thought that's what would happen.  But just as my

209

brain was sending that message to my trigger finger, one of the guys on the floor, the one from whom I had taken the bat, flung up a fist and knocked the Colt out of my grip.

Before I could go after it, big Slag was upon me. He yanked Erin out of my grip and threw her onto the floor where she landed with a yelp. I took my right fist and rammed it up into his solar plexus with all my strength. Slag chuckled as if I had gone after him with a tickle feather. He swung at me and I ducked, feeling the rush of cooling wind on my head as his fist sent my new hat flying.

I followed with a left aimed at his face, but he was so tall I missed it. Suddenly I was being picked up by my shoulders and flung into the wall. I landed on my feet but my teeth were rattling. I ducked just in time to help Slag's big bowling ball of a fist miss my face. But now he picked me up again.

This time it was in a bear hug. Only this bear didn't make nice-nice with the hugs. He was trying for damage of some kind. I thought my ribs were about to crack. My arms were pinned, but I was able to pinch the skin in his armpit hard enough that he cried out in pain. He then loosened his squeeze just enough so I was able to yank my arms free. And I really went after that ugly kisser of his with both fists flying. The fat on his face wasn't nearly as good at protecting him as the fat on his gut had been. I really pummeled him. Blowing his rotten breath at me in a painful staccato, he looked wounded – as if I had deeply hurt his feelings. He dropped and I went sprawling, looking for my gun.

I saw it and, just as I stood and made a move to retrieve it, it was kicked away.

By Blaine.

I glared at him and went to chase the gun. But I heard Slag's heavy steps behind me. Erin, coming to life, yelled, "Look out!"

Too late, I caught Slag's fist in the back of my head.

And the lights went out but good.

***

It's difficult to tell what my very next memory was. Sensations mostly. One of the first things to leak through the deep, deep blackness was the acrid stink of the reptile room.

The next sensation, perhaps, was sound: rattling through my skull was the sibilation of all those snakes. This mass hiss found the spot on the back of my noggin where Slag had clobbered me, and it made my whole head throb. The stitched-up knife wound on my arm was throbbing anew as well. I would have loved a cup of coffee and a bottle of aspirins right about then.

Instinctively, I raised a hand to my head – only to discover that neither hand was capable of obeying the command from my brain. I was tied down to a soft surface, my arms pinned tightly to my sides. My next returning sensation, touch, was telling me that I was stripped naked to the waist and that some type of rough cord was digging into my bare arms.

I opened my eyes a crack and my vision came into focus. Unfortunately, the first thing I saw was the vast and grinning mug of Slag leaning over me. A man of few words, his grin widened – showing off his moss green teeth – when he saw my eyes were open. That meaty fist of his (practically the size of my entire head) came down at me in a blur, and, oh, how Slag's eyes twinkled. It was like getting hit by a claw-foot bathtub. My brain spun inside my skull and things went dark again.

But only a moment later, before I descended too far into unconsciousness, I was dragged back to the land of light by a splash of cold water to the face. I coughed and sprayed water from my mouth. And that wasn't all. In a small gush of spit and blood, a back tooth of mine shot out from between my lips like a fat watermelon seed.

Slag stood over me chuckling as he held an empty water glass.

"Aw, Slag, you little prick," I sputtered, "that was my favorite molar!"

Slag didn't find my remark particularly funny, and he reared back his fist for another go at my face.

"Okay, Slag, that's enough," said a voice I didn't recognize, coming from behind me somewhere. "You mess up that kisser of his too much, and Hilda's only gonna get pissed at you."

This stopped Slag cold. His face turned a little pale, and he backed away from me.

The same voice said, "Go get her, Gordy. Tell her he's waking up." I heard whoever Gordy was open a door and leave the room.

I was able to raise my head a bit and I looked around the best I could. They had me tied to a cot, the kind with a thin mattress on a metal frame and not the canvas-stretched-over-a-wooden-frame kind. The cord was a very thick brown type of twine. It chafed my bare skin. So far my pants and socks were still on me, but my shoes were gone. Like my arms, my knees and ankles were tied to the cot. Not counting Gordy, it looked like there were four guys left in here with me, and they included Blaine and Slag. Slag sullenly stood nearby and hatefully glowered at me from a far corner. Blaine hovered and glanced at me now and then but avoided true eye contact.

Erin sat handcuffed to a wooden chair in another corner. Her head was lowered and she seemed to be crying again.

The recent activity with Slag had the fer-de-lances all riled up. Some were banging their heads against glass, and the noise level of the hissing was becoming unbearable.

As we waited for (I assumed) Lana, I asked Blaine, "Where'd you get all these snakes, anyway?"

Without looking at me directly, he said, "Well, Hilda had the one. And we stole some. And I've been having quite a bit of luck raising our own."

"What do you mean 'stole' some?" I said. "Where can you even find these things around here?"

"The reptile house at Lincoln Park Zoo, for one. Don't you remember reading about the break-in there a couple years ago? That was us." And he said it with some pride, as if he had invented the cheese log with shaved almonds.

"Shut up, Blaine, you're talking too much."

"No, I didn't read anything about it," I answered Blaine, anyway. "I was in Germany."

"You shut your mouth too, you fuckin' Mick," said the voice. "You've caused enough trouble in here tonight."

And he moved into view, raising his open hand to me in warning. And I recognized him. He was the Asian kid I'd seen looking at us through Lana's bedroom window. The one I'd chased, Cappy's friend. That meant perhaps that he had come with Cappy in an attempt to murder Lana. If so, it might mean that he was another of Blaine's rebellious allies. On the other hand, he might also think I was responsible for Cappy getting killed – and that was sadly the truth, though I had been protecting Lana from an intruder at the time. I had no idea she was going to kill him. But it did mean that if this guy were a friend of Cappy's, yet still lived, then Lana had not gotten a good look at his face at the window and still thought of him as loyal (or at least possibly loyal).

Curiously, all these guys – including Blaine, Slag, and even the guy still outside tied-up with garden hose – wore similar shirts but in varying colors. Shiny, bowling-type shirts. I wondered if this were Lana's idea of a uniform, so her men could be easily identified visually. Zombie fatigues. I thought about asking, felt the bloody hole where my tooth used to be, and thought better of it. Maybe it was a question for which the answer was not worth getting my face bashed.

For a few minutes we quietly waited, the only sounds being that infernal hiss and Erin's muffled sobs. The pit of her misery seemed bottomless.

Finally, there was some noise out in the hall, and in through the door came a dark-haired guy I assumed was Gordy, and he was followed by Lana.

She had on a peeled-down version of her gypsy get-up. The turban was still there, as were the hoop earrings, and the gray wig (a beautifully coifed hairpiece, not some Halloween monstrosity), but her dress was now more modern, knee-length with a plunging neckline, more in keeping with the madam of a brothel than a storefront palm reader – and cooler too for this stifling building. She still wore jangly bracelets and a collection of rings on her fingers. One piece of jewelry I had spotted previously, however, during our little *tete-a-tete* on the loveseat. It was that pendant, the large polished stone of some kind, black with odd streaks of color.  As it dangled from a gold chain, it bobbed in and out of that cleavage.

She smiled at me, but instead of a greeting, she said to the guy from the window, "Gag him, will you!"  She used a pretty phony-sounding Eastern European accent I had never heard from her so far.

Immediately, I felt some rag being stuffed into my mouth and tied in place.  I growled but it was done with efficiency.  It seemed an odd way to start this meeting off, but maybe she didn't want me blabbing about her accent and disguise to any minions present who might believe her act to be genuine.

Still using the accent, she finally addressed me directly.  "In a little while," she said, grinning, "when you are in a more cooperative state of mind, maybe you can shed some light for me about the current whereabouts of our doorman, Chico.  He has gone missing."  She turned to Gordy and said, "Go watch the door.  Arm yourself with a pistol, your switchblade will not be adequate.  Watch out for friends of his trying to sneak in with the paying customers."

"Yes, Madame Hilda," said Gordy, and he left the room.

Holy crap.

Lana slowly turned her attention back to me. She studied me for a bit, maybe weighing her words before she spoke. Finally she said: "I tried to bring you into the fold easily, you know. But you just wouldn't have it. You resisted at every turn, just when I thought I had you. But – well, I'm a patient woman. And determined. I knew I would get you, once I knew I had to have you. And I knew that the first time I laid eyes on you. It's a shame I have to use such force. But it's your own fault. I can't have you coming in here like you did. Charging in like a bull." She smirked. "Expecting to get your way. It's an admirable quality all right. But I need to turn that around right now and make that quality work for me. This is my world you have charged into. And the only one who gets their way here is me." She smirked that practiced smirk yet again. "But you'll find that out in just a few moments."

Again, the only sounds, as Lana surveyed the room, were the hissing and Erin's tearful sobs (which had become intermittent). Lana looked over at Erin with annoyance and said, to no one in particular, "Shut that one up. I can't think."

There was, at once, a loud slap and Erin was silenced. I went crazy, straining at my bonds and rattling my cot.

"Settle down, mister," said Lana. "I'll have to deal with Little Red later tonight. Don't make it worse for her." I was furious but I calmed myself for Erin's sake.

Lana walked over to a small lamp on a shelf, next to a terrarium that contained a frighteningly huge fer-de-lance. She tested the length of the lamp's extension cord by pulling it in my direction. Satisfied that it was big enough, she switched the lamp on and set it on a table near the foot of my cot.

"Slag," she said, "turn off that overhead light."

Slag obeyed at once, clearly eager to please his mistress. The room became quite dark except for the little lamp and a few odd lights situated over certain terrariums.

"Kill those snake lights, Blaine." Dutifully, Blaine began shutting off the terrarium lights one by one. Soon, the only illumination in the room came from the small lamp.

I didn't want to become a zombie. But if life has taught me anything – just like when our troop transport passed through the Panama Canal in the middle of the night and I became an unwilling participant in the Pacific Theater of War – sometimes, even though you don't want to become a zombie, you become a zombie anyway.

Lana grabbed a small stool from under a table, and she set it down on the floor to the left of my cot. She sat on it, and I now had a perfect view of her from the waist up. She leaned over me and grabbed the lamp and readjusted it. Then she fiddled with the shade till it almost acted like a spotlight. Half her face (her left side) was brightly illuminated as were her left shoulder, left arm, and left breast. Her other half was obscured in the inkiest of shadows.

I tried struggling just a bit more. It was pointless. In fact, my performance made Lana chuckle.

"You are not going anywhere, my dolly," she said, still committed to that ridiculous accent. (I suddenly realized she must be aping Maria Ouspenskaya who played the old gypsy in *The Wolf Man*.) Then, from somewhere in her bosom, Lana produced a large hypodermic needle with a small cork stuck on the point. The glass of the syringe was filled an orange-yellow liquid that might have been the urine of a very sick farm animal.

Okay, this was not funny anymore.

Lana saw my eyes widen at the sight of the needle and she chuckled again.

"This, my love, is the genuine article," she said, holding the needle closer to my face so I could get a good look at it. "Some very helpful nature-types taught me to make it. It's incredible. You can get all the ingredients from the grocery and the pharmacy. A little of this, a little of that. Some intense heat, and – well, the chemistry is quite impressive. Works amazingly well. You had a little last night in your bourbon, you know. Doesn't always work as well orally, but I think it would have this time if you'd been cooperative. Sadly," she said with a mock frown, "you weren't."

Yeah, I thought, Blaine told me that you also need a shot of the fer-de-lance venom. And then I also thought that maybe she did have one of those things slithering around her apartment after all.

"Alcohol swab, Blaine," she said, and there was good old Blaine wiping a bare area on my twine-bound bicep with an alcohol-soaked cotton ball. Good old Blaine. I wanted to autograph his nose with my knuckles.

Next, Lana removed the cork from the needle, she flicked some non-existent bubbles from the side of the glass, and she squirted a tiny amount of the liquid into the air and onto the floor, thus filling the needle.

And, without hesitating a moment longer, she jabbed me with that thing, right into the spot Blaine had cleaned, emptying the farm animal urine into my own personal body. It burned like hell.

Well, at least they were sanitary around this joint.

"Ah, fuck!" I yelled into my gag so no one could understand me.

Lana lit a cigarette as we waited. Slowly, slowly, the burning feeling disappeared. It was replaced by a calming euphoria. Lana smoked a few minutes and finished her cigarette, then stubbed it out in a nearby ashtray.

"That should be enough time," she said in a low key whisper. I had never found her voice so soothing before. "Here comes a good part. I really think you're going to like it." What I hadn't gotten used to yet was Lana's keen sense of irony.

Very slowly, she removed her pendant from around her neck. She held it up to my face.

"This, dearest, is Honduran opal. Look at it," she purred. "Beautiful, isn't it?"

She held the chain between thumb and forefinger and spun the stone slowly. She brought the opal close to my eyes, but not too close. I was just able to focus on it before it would have gotten all blurry.

A small alarm went off in the back of my mind. A tiny voice in the wilderness. It told me not to look at the stone any longer, that I would be in danger if I did.

I squeezed my eyes shut.

"Oh, don't close your eyes, darling," Lana purred. "The show is just about to get interesting." When I didn't immediately obey, she added in the same accented purr, "Don't make me have them force your eyes open. It isn't nearly as much fun. I know you won't like those uncomfortable clamps."

It never came to that. I could tell my willpower had indeed been compromised. But she was right. I didn't like the idea of eyelid clamps.

"That's my good baby. Now watch the stone."

And I did watch the stone as it spun slowly in one direction then another. It was like the spinning of the Earth on its axis – if the Earth slowed down and then spun the opposite direction every few seconds, making Japan the Land of the Rising Sun and the Land of the Setting Sun, over and over and over again…

But the Honduran opal wasn't exactly round and planet-shaped. It was shaped more like a fat pear or a fat teardrop. It hung from its skinny end which was sunk into an elaborate gold setting, attached by glue or tiny drilled holes or some other unseen method. I continued to watch the spin of it.

I sank into a reverie. Honestly, my memory of this part was like a visit to Paradise. This part.

"Look at the opal," Lana's whispering purr nudged itself into my reverie. "Look at it. It's the deepest, darkest black you will ever find on Earth. But not only black. You see the streaks of color, don't you? So many unusual colors. This is what drew me to it in that Honduran marketplace to begin with. Look at the colors, Watch them spin."

I did look at the colors. I did watch them spin. Purty colors.

"Red streaks. Blue streaks. Yellow streaks. Green streaks. Purple and orange. The longer you look, the more you see. Fine, fine streaks of color.

Fine as hair. Finer than hair. Some as fine as tiny cracks. It isn't a black opal at all. Is it?"

"No, it isn't," I heard myself trying to answer through the gag.

"Would you like the gag out of your mouth?"

"Mm-hm."

"Are you going to be good?"

"Mm-hm."

"Blaine?" she said in the same purr without breaking the mood. I felt Blaine untie the gag and pull the rag from my mouth, which felt dry as a tortoise carcass in the Mojave. But it didn't seem to matter. I didn't ask for water, and none was offered.

After a bit of time that could have been one minute or twenty minutes, Lana said. "Watch the streaks of color. Do you see the streaks of color?"

"Yes," I replied.

"From now on," she said, kicking the purr up to a new feline level, "when you answer me, start saying 'yes, Madame Hilda' or 'no, Madame Hilda,' understand?"

"Yes, Madame Hilda," I said. It seemed like the thing to say, under the circumstances. I mean, it's what the woman wanted to be called.

"That's my good boy," she said, and she could not keep the smugness out of her voice.

"Look closer. Deeper. Into the opal," she continued. "The streaks of color. You see them?"

"Yes, Madame Hilda."

"But there are not only streaks of color, are there?"

"No, Madame Hilda."

"No. Not at all. Especially near the bottom of the opal. You see it, don't you? A big splash of color. See it?"

"Yes, Madame Hilda."

"A huge splash. A flare-up, realy. Like a burst of flame. It's all the colors of fire, isn't it? White, red, orange – and yellow. You see it, don't you?"

"Yes, Madame Hilda." I had, of course, been fixated on that splash of color she'd mentioned. It kept spinning around, first one way, then the other – like that big red spot on the planet Jupiter.

"Think of that fiery splash. Think of those flames. Their unrelenting heat, like the flames of Hell."

"Yes, Madame Hilda."

There was another pause and, as I continued watching the spinning opal, I felt myself relaxing more, going deeper into the reverie.

When at last she spoke again, Lana said, "I'm going to talk to you very personally now, Bobber. And I'm going to call you by name. Understand, Bobber?"

"Yes, Madame Hilda."

A shorter pause. Then: "Bobber – when I first saw you yesterday I, well, I knew you were the man for me."

What? What's that then?

She hadn't asked me a question, though, so I held my tongue. And I continued to watch the spinning opal.

"Yes, I knew you were the man for me. I knew I had to have you. But you played hard-to-get. And that's not going to work. You know I always get what I want, don't you?"

"Yes, Madame Hilda."

"And I want you. And now I'm going to tell you a little secret. You want me as well. Now you do. Don't you?"

"Yes, Madame Hilda." My mother didn't raise a fool. And yet, I did wonder what would happen if I tried not to answer her, not to call her

Madame Hilda. I was pretty sure I could stop – it just didn't seem like a good time to try.

"I'll tell you something else, Bobber. Listen to me, Bobber. I own you now. And from now on, the thought of disobeying me or defying me will make your insides burn with the flame of the opal. Disobeying me will cast your soul into Hell, and you will burn forever. The pain will be everlasting and greater than anything you have ever endured. Do you understand?"

"Yes, Madame Hilda." I mean now we were going into familiar territory for me. As stated, I was raised Catholic, and the nuns would delight in scaring us shitless (during catechism class) with tales of mortal sin and eternal damnation. All this, however, seemed slightly blasphemous. But I still didn't think it was a good idea to disagree with Lana in the present circumstance.

"Belonging to me," she continued to purr, "body and soul, is the only way you can ever rule at my side, and own all of this with me. Do you understand?"

Hmm, an offer to rule all this with her side by side? Was I hearing wedding bells? But I did wonder how someone like Slag was taking in all this. Of course, maybe she had made a similar offer to everyone in this room. I couldn't be sure, but I didn't think so. It sounded like she really did have grand designs for me.

And so it went. She took me deeper and deeper into the reverie – her trance, if you will, repeating the same things over again at each level. Finally, it felt like I'd really been asleep, deeply asleep, when she said in her whispered purr:

"Okay, Blaine. I think we're ready for the venom injection."

Lana sat back and lit another cigarette. She smoked quietly while Blaine did the honors. He swabbed my right arm this time (the one facing away from Lana). I wanted to make my voice say something like, 'no, Blaine, a thousand times no,' or words to that effect. But for some reason, even though I was no longer gagged, I couldn't make myself say a damn thing.

Blaine produced a hypodermic needle of his own, and injected me in the right arm. Had he given me the old "saline instead of venom" treatment? Or was he truly a turncoat out to save his own skin? I didn't know. Perhaps I was doomed to be a zombie – or, at least, a slave of Lana's.

But, there in the near darkness, something else happened.

Lana was inhaling a lungful of smoke, and Blaine was fussing over my right arm, daubing up blood. And just as Lana exhaled with a slight whooshing sound, I felt one of the pieces of twine binding my right bicep quietly pop. Had it been cut? And all at once I felt all the twine loosen its grip on me at all spots – as if I had been tied to the cot with one continuous length. And, almost at the same moment, I felt Blaine press something into my right hand, out of Lana's line of vision,

It was my pen knife.

Good old Blaine.

I had to be very careful to play this advantage (if that's what it turned out to be). Lana continued to smoke casually and didn't seem to suspect a thing. Neither did anyone else.

At last she stubbed out this most recent cigarette and said, "All right, you're ready for the door to the kingdom. The final step. I must admit, I'm looking forward to this."

She stood slowly then began to remove some of her bracelets, reaching over me to place them and the Honduran opal pendant on the table, between the lamp and the ashtray. As she did so, she said in very low, throaty tones, "You just behave now. Understand? I promise you will like this next part too." She looked me over carefully, and added, "Well I'm not going to untie you. Not yet. Not even your knees and ankles. Not sure a hundred percent yet if I can trust you completely. But that's coming." She smirked and tugged at my belt buckle. "We will just yank your trousers down to your thighs. It will all work out just fine." And she moved to unzip her dress.

What, in here? I thought, in front of the gang? In front of Erin?

But even as I thought this, the gang began to gather around us in a tight circle, their faces masks of blatant lust (all but Slag's face which was a mask of hatred and jealousy – towards me). So, this was how it worked, huh. This was one of the ways she kept the troops entertained, by letting them gather 'round and witness each "new guy" get brought into the fold.

She abandoned her zipper for a moment. Never taking her hungry eyes off me (the wounded gazelle bleeding on the veldt), Lana laid her hoop earrings on the table as well, then went back to fiddling with the dress zipper tab, behind her neck.

It was time to act. The problem was, I wasn't sure what to do.

Gordy spared me the trouble.

From the open door, his silhouette barely visible, his voice broke the spell of seduction: "Pardon me, Madame Hilda," he said, "I am really so very sorry!"

Lana spun on the kid with a temper that was truly terrifying. "God damn it, Gordy, what is it? Can't you see the important business I have here? Go on, spit it out!"

"Like I said, Madame Hilda," said Gordy, tripping all over his words, "I'm so very sorry. I see your important business. But that one man, that Ferguson man, the one you said we should never turn away? He's downstairs and wants a girl for the night."

"So get him a girl!" Lana spat.

"But, Madame Hilda. He wants this one. Over there. Little Red. He asked for her specifically. I told him she was sick, but he didn't care. He twisted my arm pretty damn bad. Thought he was gonna pull it off me."

"Crap," Lana said under her breath. "All right, Blaine, run and get my make-up bag, I'd better doll her up." She looked at me and said,

"Don't worry. We'll finish playing later, even if I have to do everything over."

She strode over to the light switch and the room was once again flooded by the glow of the overhead. It was clear that money trumped all when it came to her desires.

"Go back down, Gordy, and tell Mr. Ferguson that Little Red will be right with him. Put him in the second parlor. Give him some liquor."

I hated that they called Erin "Little Red."

"Yes, Madame Hilda," Gordy said and disappeared back out the door.

"She's not cooperative tonight, Madame Hilda," said the kid I'd seen at the window.

"Like how, Charlie?" So, his name was Charlie.

"She put up a huge fight when we caught the Mick over there trying to take her away."

"Hm. She is due for a treatment. We can't have her gouging out the eyes of a paying customer that pays as much as Ferguson does." She paused slightly, and I could see the gears were really turning in her brain. "All right," she said at last, "she just had another dose of my serum last week.

That should be enough to protect her. We'll give her a quick treatment. Blaine!"

"You sent him for your make-up bag, Madame Hilda," said Charlie.

"Right. Okay, Slag. You like to play with the snakes, you've done this. Go get that big monster next to you there. Don't get killed. Bring it over to Little Red and let it bite her on the wrist."

"No!" Erin squealed.

"Be quiet," said Lana dismissively. You won't die… probably."

"Yes, Madame Hilda," said Slag. And, with slight difficulty, he pulled on one of the big leather gloves over his giant hand. I imagined no matter how often they were injected with Lana's serum, they were still always in danger of getting an accidental overdose of venom, just working with the snakes.

Next, Slag lifted the lid off the terrarium, and, using a metal tool – a rod with a flat bend at its end – he began fishing around in there, trying to pin the head of the huge serpent.

All eyes were on Slag as he did this, and no one was watching me. I tugged my right bicep up and the twine came loose, but it didn't come off. I was able, however, to slip my arm free. If I'd had the time, I would have been able to pull the whole works free. But I didn't have time. So with my newly liberated hand, I opened my pen knife and began cutting twine. The sharp blade moved through the ragged cord easily. I worked my way down, keeping one eye on my work and the other on the others. First I freed my left bicep, then my left knee, then my right knee, then my right ankle.

I was just starting on my left ankle when Erin screamed again. Slag had captured the snake and, holding it tightly behind the head, he walked, grinning, towards Erin, the serpent angrily coiling and uncoiling itself around his arm.

Instinctively, I tried to pull my left ankle loose, and I only pulled the twine tighter. Making myself take a quick, calming breath (something for which I didn't have time), I cut through the twine and freed my left ankle. Erin screamed yet again, and I saw that Slag had pulled her free arm up and was bringing his other hand – which held the struggling fer-de-lance – close to the raised wrist.

Making my cramped and drugged legs obey me, I vaulted off the cot and sprang onto the table next to Slag. Before anybody could do anything about it, I firmly yanked the snake by the tail and pulled it out of Slag's grip. In one motion, I flung the reptile back over my shoulder where I heard it crash into something glass and someone took the Lord's name in vain.

Slag blinked, confused. On the table, I now had a much better advantage over him. Before he could engage his brain, I slammed him with my fist putting all the weight I had into it. This time, I found that wonderful spot on his chin that no amount of fat can protect, and he fell with a meteoric crash, hitting a table first and sending lab equipment flying and shattering. The tip of his tongue, bitten off, popped out of his mouth.

I looked down at Erin, who was staring wild-eyed at me. Seeing where she was handcuffed, and in the rush of the moment, I grabbed the back of the chair and broke it off in splinters, freeing her.

"Come on," I said, "let's move."

Before we got very far, Lana was standing there holding a gun. It was Pa's Colt.

"No. Don't move," she said. Her smirk gone, there was only anger in her eyes. "No matter how much I like you," she said, "you're always doing something to piss me off. I'm afraid I've changed my mind about you."

Three of her flunkies were still conscious, and they may or may not have been on my side. Blaine,

Charlie, and a guy whose name I hadn't yet learned. They moved in around Lana in a protective formation.

Suddenly, there was a great ruckus up the stairs and into the little hall. Lana and everyone else turned to look.

Through the door burst in Peggy O'Kief, her brother Colin, and a whole lot of other O'Kiefs and O'Kief friends. And, by God, even Ma's face was in there! They froze in and near the doorway when they saw the gun in Lana's hand.

Lana must have gotten the sense of what was happening right away, because she said, cool as nothing else in this room, "Don't anyone come any closer or I'll shoot them both."

Lana walked up to us and deftly grabbed Erin by the back of the hair.

"You're coming with me, Red," she spat and pulled Erin out of my grip. I watched paralyzed, our crowd of rescuers doing likewise in the doorway.

She looked over at Slag who hulked nearby, tears of pain running down his cheeks, blood running down his chin, the tip of his tongue cradled in an outstretched hand.

"I'll sew that back on for you, stupid," Lana said – and the hurt on Slag's face reflected the emotional hurt in her words. "Go get the motorboat ready. Red and I will be right out. Take a snake in a bag with you!"

Wordlessly, Slag put his tongue-tip in his pocket, grabbed a cloth bag and thrust another of the bigger monsters into it – and left the room.

When he'd gone, Lana said to the rest of us, "Here's how it's gonna work. You all are staying right here or I'll put a bullet into the head of your little babycakes." She twisted the handful of Erin's hair and Erin squealed in terror and pain. I glanced over at the O'Kief's, and Colin's eyes were wild with rage. But there wasn't a thing we could do.

At least I didn't think so.

I looked over into the frantic faces of the O'Kiefs and saw something amazing. Peggy was crammed in there and she had very quietly been pulling a bobby pin – slingshot style with a green rubber band – between her thumb and forefinger (the way we would shoot things at each other as kids). You fool, I thought, this woman is serious about hurting your sister, do you want to get Erin killed?

It was then that Lana stuck the gun right in my face. "I see you trying to signal over there," she said. "None of – !" It was then that Peggy let the bobby pin fly. Her aim was deadly accurate.

Lana cried out as Peggy's projectile smacked her smartly on the wrist. The gun went off, pinwheeling inches from my nose, with a loud echoing *crack*. Another terrarium shattered. My cheek felt warm from the near collision with a bullet.

A figure stepped swiftly through the crowd and landed a beautiful right cross on Lana's face that sent her sprawling. I'll be damned if the right cross didn't belong to Ma. She rubbed her sore fist as the others rushed in for Erin.

I plopped down on the seat of the shattered chair that Erin had been occupying – it still had legs and had become a stool.

I was reeling from the appearance of this neighborhood cavalry. I wanted to both congratulate Peggy for coming to the rescue as she had, but also scold her for taking the chance she did with that bobby pin. For now I kept my yap shut.

There was a whole lot of back-slapping and gleeful cooing going on around Erin. We really should have known better than to let our guards down.

Before there was time to think, Slag appeared in the other doorway. He no longer held the bag with the snake or his tongue-tip. He held another gun – a bigger one than Pa's Colt.

Seeing Lana moaning on the floor his face went red. Her gray wig and turban – as well as a little cap made from the top of a nylon stocking – lay next to her head, exposing her mussed blonde hair.

Slag pulled her to her feet and she said, rubbing her chin, "I'll be fine. Get Red, we're still taking her."

Without blinking, Slag plucked Erin out of our midst and in a moment the three of them – Lana, Slag, and Erin – were gone.

I stood, still mostly bare-skinned in my pants and socks, the adrenaline pumping through me.

"Okay, she really wants Erin alive, that's clear," I said in a low voice, trying to command order out of well-meaning chaos. "Let me go after them – there's a little boat dock right outside here. You can all follow, but be quiet about it. She might want Erin alive, but we also don't want to make that Lana any angrier. She's a very dangerous person – a killer. And keep a lookout for any other thugs who work here. They've probably fled by now, after that gunshot, but you never know."

I had their attention, even hot-headed Colin. "Also, there are some other women – not sure how many – that can also use some rescuin' on the floor above."

"We got that, Bobber," said Patrick O'Kief, another of Erin's brothers, nodding at me. He and Peewee and some O'Kief cousin disappeared out the door in which they had come.

"And everybody watch out for loose snakes! Those things are deadly!"

I picked up Pa's Colt from the floor and headed after Lana.

This part of the house was new to me, mostly poorly lit corridors and closed doors. Somewhere in here might be that guy who was supposed to be waiting to see Erin – with any luck on our part he had heard the ruckus and also had beat it out of there. If we had to deal with him we would. But right now, I had to find that little boat dock.

With a general sense of what way the front of the building was and what way the back, I swiftly picked my way till I came to a door that I felt surely opened out onto the dock. I wasted no time and opened it a crack.

It did.

The first thing to hit me was the river smell. There was the concrete river wall right outside the door and below that the little concrete dock I had been pitched from just the night before.

And there was the motorboat.

And in the motorboat were Lana, Slag, and Erin. Slag was just casting off from the concrete dock. He still held the gun in his hand, but he didn't have it pointed at anyone.

I turned around and could see Colin and the others down at the end of the hall, waiting for some signal from me. I held my finger up for them to stay where they were and then put the same finger to my lips, hoping they would also keep quiet. It was a lot to ask.

I soundlessly stepped out onto the top of the river wall. I pulled off my socks. The cold rusty rungs of the ladder bit into my bare feet as I swiftly descended to the dock. Slag had started the outboard motor mounted on the back of the boat, Lana sat in the center, and Erin was up in the bow. She was the only one looking at me.

Just as they were about to roar away, I shouted, "Wait! Lana, please!"

The heads of Lana and Slag spun towards me. Lana barked, "Hold it one second, Slag!"

Slag cut the motor and they rocked in place. He fixed me with the most grotesque grimace of hatred, the streaks of blood still visible on his chin.

I was holding the gun pointed down.

"What is it, Bobber? I meant what I said about killing her."

"I know," I answered, trying to make my voice as sincere as possible. "They're all waiting for me in there. Leave Erin here. Take me. I… want to go with you. I really do."

"You do?" I could tell I had her interest, but I knew I was playing with dynamite.

"Yes, God damn it. I don't think I can bear to have you disappear from my life. That being king to your queen? I think I could go for it."

I could tell Slag wasn't liking this turn of events at all – his shoulders heaved. But Lana was nibbling at the hook.

"I'll tell you what, my dear. Why don't you get in the boat? I'll take you and Red both. We have to be able to make some cash to start clean.

Yes. Lay your gun down and get in the boat, dearest."

I never had time to figure out a reply. Suddenly something hit Lana in the face and she screamed. Slag had snapped. No amount of Madame Hilda's mind control could hold it in. The poor jealous hulk had flung the snake at Lana's head. And now he had taken the serpent by its ends and was strangling Lana with it.

Erin screamed as the motorboat pitched violently. I did lay down the gun and dove into the water.

The next second, I came up sputtering filth right next to the rocking boat. Slag stood, hauling the choking Lana up by the neck, the "living status" of the fer-de-lance currently undetermined.

I pulled myself up on the edge of the boat, grabbed Erin by the wrist, and yanked her into the water with me. Lifting her head above the surface, she spat miserably with a "yeep!" We turned and I guided her back to the dock.

Just as I hoped, they were all waiting for us.

"Don't worry, Erin," said Colin, lifting her single-handedly out of the water, " we ain't gonna let go of yer again."

As I climbed the ladder with the help of my neighbors, there was a great splash behind me. I twisted around and saw the motorboat had capsized. Slag and Lana continued to struggle, but now they were in the water.

Once completely onto the dock, I shivered.

The others were climbing the river wall ladder, heading back into the house, content to let Slag and Lana fight it out without our interference. I warned them about a possible encounter with Ferguson.

"We'll regroup inside – some room where there are no snakes," I said. "Basically, if you find anyone who hasn't been smart enough to get out of here by now – well, let's detain them."

As Ma walked by me, I said, "By the way, Ma, nice right cross!"

She rolled her eyes ruefully and said, "That banshee had Pa's Colt stuck right in yer face." Her brogue was dialed up to maximum intensity. "If anyone around here is gonna pull a gun on *my* kid, it'll be *me*."

She climbed the wall and went inside.

"I love yer mother," said Peggy.

She and I were the last ones on the dock. I looked out at the water for Slag and Lana – but they were gone.  One second the boat floundered sideways in the river, and then – bloop! – it was gone also.

"Jaysus," said Peggy.  "Should we try to save them?"

Sick at the thought of the task, nevertheless, I said, "I suppose we should," and made a move to jump back into the drink.

Peggy's arms were suddenly around my waist in a vice-like grip.

"Are you crazy, Man?  I think I was just kidding!  Nature is taking its course."

I stopped moving towards the water and let the warmth of Peggy's body flow into me.  It felt damn good.  I waited to see if I felt guilty at all.  Sadly, for Lana's and Slag's sakes, no such emotion came to me.

Finally, I sighed a little and said, "God help us, but I think you're right, Peggy.  Not sure any rescue attempt is safe, anyway – they've got that deadly snake floating around with them.  If it's still alive, one bite from that thing and a rescuer would be dead.  And then what would you have?"

"Well," Peggy said, tightening her grip, "I'm right and you are not going back in there.  Sorry I brought it up."

My teeth were chattering, but we just stood there for a minute or two. It felt great not having someone trying to kill me. Peggy's warmth kept flowing into me, though. Finally, I broke the spell somewhat and picked up the Colt.

"Don't want to leave this behind."

"Hey, I almost forgot," said Peggy. She reached into her blouse and pulled out something she had tucked into her bra. "I found this on a counter in that snake room. Is it anything?"

Dangling from her hand, on its chain, was the Honduran Opal.

"Holy crap," I said. "Yeah, it's something all right. But I'm not sure how to explain it. It's a Honduran opal and it belonged to Lana. Yes, that Lana. I'm tempted just to chuck it into the river after her. But I suppose you should hold onto it for a while. The police might want to look at it."

"The police? We gonna report all this, huh?"

"I'm thinking we should."

"I mean, do we really have to?" Peggy asked. "We can't just go home? The police would never know what happened here with these scum, and we would never have to get involved."

"I'll admit it's tempting," I said. "But there could be all kinds of clues around here – and back at Lana's place – that might tie me to these events. Remember poor dead Cappy? There's also a guy who worked for Lana running around with a piece of paper with my autograph. And who knows what else? And there are the families of those other girls – who were prisoners alongside Erin – and they deserve answers to questions that maybe only I could provide. No, I'd rather be seen as someone providing answers than as someone who was trying to make tracks, so to speak."

"I guess you're right."

"We can hash it all out inside. Why don't you stow that pendant back in its hiding place?" I said, indicating the opal.

Peggy stuffed it back into her bra with a demure smile.

"I hope we can find the makings for a pot of coffee in there," she said.

"Before I forget," I said, "you were fantastic tonight – the way you mustered the troops. What a rescue!"

"Thanks. It was nerve-wracking. After I called Colin, I thought it would take them forever to get here. I gave them the address but it's so dark! They came in three cars. Good thing they had your yellow car to look for. You know it's way after midnight."

"I had no idea what time it was. My hands were full. Say – I'm surprised your parents didn't come."

"Oh, they're here. Dad kept talking about killing someone so we made him stay in the car. And it was Mom's job to guard him. But wait till they hear what you did for Erin! They'll have you dipped in bronze or something. Seriously, Bobber. You saved her. You figured it all out and saved her! My family will always be in your debt." And she kissed me hard on the lips. That went a good deal further to warm me up than even coffee might've..

"Wow. I mean, after, I just…"

"Yer turnin' blue with the cold, Kid," said Peggy. "Let's get you inside."

We moved together in the direction of the river wall ladder. But my leg was caught on something. I turned to free it so I could get the hell inside. The problem was my right ankle. Only it wasn't caught on something, it was caught in something.

It was the meaty grip of Slag.

He had pulled himself partway up the shorter dock ladder. He didn't look at all well. He was soaking wet – and that's not all. The huge fer-de-lance had attached itself to his face (his left cheek, to be precise) by its fangs. Whether it was in the throes of death or it was merely feeling frisky, the snake curled and uncurled tighter and tighter around Slag's substantial neck.

I pulled with all my might to free myself from his grip, but I couldn't budge an inch. And my pal seemed less intent on using me to pull himself out of the water as he seemed to want to pull me into the river with him.

My foot skidded toward the edge of the dock as Slag let himself go limp.

Peggy was grunting in panicky gasps as she tried to pull me by the waist in the opposite direction. It felt as though if she were to let go of me for only a moment I would go right into the icy water. I still had the Colt in my hand and, instead of squeezing off a shot at Slag's head as I should have, I swung the barrel at his skull in an attempt to knock him cold. The gun merely glanced off the hard noggin and skittered out of my grip and onto the concrete out of my grasp. In the dim light from the bare bulbs that illuminated this little dock,

I could see Slag's eyes squinting at me with hideous glee.

I slipped a little closer to the edge.

"Can you get up the ladder?" I said to Peggy. "Can you open the door, call the others?"

"I'll try," she gasped. But she only let go with one hand for a second and I went sliding right up to the edge. Peggy screamed and redid her grip on me, tighter than ever. I hated to think it, but I was surely going in with Slag and Peggy was going to follow.

Slag seemed to be mostly back in the water, his arms outstretched, both fists gripping my right ankle now. Peggy tried to kick at his hands but couldn't get purchase.

I stared into Slag's bizarrely hateful eyes. "Here we go," I said through clenched teeth.

And suddenly, the eyes rolled back in his head. I felt his hands go limp on my ankle. And just like that, he slid silently back below the surface of the Chicago River. I guess the fer-de-lance had finally pumped enough venom into Slag's face.

Peggy and I collapsed onto the dock and into each others' arms.

After taking only a couple minutes to catch our breath, we scrambled to our feet, I grabbed the gun, and we got up the wall and inside.

I shut the door behind us and turned the deadbolt lock.

Peggy and I looked at each other – and we laughed. Maybe it was a slightly hysterical laugh.

Finally catching her breath, Peggy said, "But, you know, seriously, maybe this is what you should do for a living."

"I'll have to think about that one, Peg," I said.

And we went to find the others, the rest of my clothes, and maybe some coffee. But it was already warmer.

## The End